# HELP WANTED

# HELP WANTED

*Short Stories about
Young People Working*

Selected by

## ANITA SILVEY

LITTLE, BROWN AND COMPANY

Boston    New York    Toronto    London

First Edition

The characters and events portrayed in this book are fictitious. Any similarity to real persons, living or dead, is coincidental and not intended by the authors.

Copyright acknowledgments appear on page 173.

Library of Congress Cataloging-in-Publication Data

Help wanted : short stories about young people working / selected by Anita Silvey.
　　　　p.　　cm.
　　Summary: A collection of twelve short stories exploring the world of work, by such authors as Gary Soto, Norma Fox Mazer, and Ray Bradbury.
　　ISBN 0-316-79148-2
　　1. Work — Juvenile fiction.　2. Short stories, American. [1. Work — Fiction.　2. Short stories.]　I. Silvey, Anita.
PZ5.H359　1997
[Fic] — dc20　　　　　　　　　　　　　　　　96-34827

10　9　8　7　6　5　4　3　2　1

MV-NY

Published simultaneously in Canada by Little, Brown & Company (Canada) Limited

Printed in the United States of America

To my husband, Bill Clark
As Bernie always said, "You are something else."

— A. S.

# Contents

# Selecter's Note

Sigmund Freud once told us that all we have is love and work. Both are part of the adolescent years. But while we have endless books for young people about love, work has been shamelessly ignored.

Work became part of my own life in my adolescent years. My first position was in the teenage apparel department of Sears, Roebuck. Now, I was a teenage slob — more interested in reading books than in reading fashion magazines. My mother must have helped me dress appropriately for the interview, and somehow or other I got through it. And then day after long summer's day, I tried — unkempt and fashionless — to help young women make purchases of clothes. I didn't care about clothes, didn't deal well with the public; after a few hours on the job, I was often found hiding in the bathroom, crying. My supervisors talked to me about my unappealing dress; they criticized my shyness. Not surprisingly, I was not invited back to Sears the next summer. I ended up working for the parks department, reading stories to children. Unbeknownst to me, because of my failure in fashion, I stumbled upon my life's work.

Sometimes we are fortunate enough to discover our careers in our adolescent years; sometimes it takes much longer. But, inevitably, we have to begin the process of finding what we will do — and dealing with the emotional consequences of work.

*Help Wanted* contains a dozen stories about young people and work. The protagonists of these stories take jobs for a variety of reasons. Some seek employment because of their passion, or what they care about, as Cherylene Lee describes in "Hollywood and the Pits." Some, like T.J. in "Antaeus," work because they are driven to, because they enjoy it. Some work for extra money, or a treasured object, as in Ray Bradbury's "Dandelion Wine." Some work because it is a necessity; they must help provide food for themselves and for their family, as in Francisco Jiménez's "The Circuit."

But for whatever reason young people work, the rewards are often very different from those they expected, as Michael Dorris demonstrates in "The Original Recipe" or Tim Wynne-Jones in "Hard Sell." No matter why these young people get a job, they are all changed because of it. All grow in different ways because of their efforts.

Some of the stories in this collection, such as Budge Wilson's "Be-ers and Doers," are serious and passionate; some, such as "QWERTYUIOP," are light and funny. Some are included to make us all think about how and why we work; some are included to help us think about how and why others, from different backgrounds and families from our own, might view employment.

The poet Marge Piercy wrote, "The pitcher cries for water to carry / and a person for work that is real." We all start hunting for work that is real — sometimes as very young people, sometimes only when we are older. These stories are offered with the hope that they may help young readers as they begin that journey.

*Anita Silvey*
*Boston, Massachusetts*

# Selecter's Acknowledgments

Several young readers looked over the proposed contents of the book and much improved the final volume. Thanks go to Maeve Visser Knoth and the students of Buckingham Browne and Nichols School, in Cambridge, Massachusetts, as well as the fifth, sixth, and seventh graders at the Tower School in Marblehead, Massachusetts, and their teachers Georgia Sledge and Carol Grey and librarian Nancy Vasilakis.

I am particularly indebted to the students at Greenville Middle School, in Greenville, South Carolina. Their librarian Pat Scales and their teachers Tom Edwards and Leigh Sumerel not only sent on their comments but also arranged for me to talk to these young readers as well. I hope they learned half as much from the process as I did. So special thanks go to Richard Allen, Kelly Anastes, Tyler Cooper, Beth Ewoldsen, Justin Hayes, Katherine Horton, Eddie Hunter, Chris Martin, Melissa Moose, Brian Nelson, Laura Noel, Kelly Paterson, Walker Pickering, Sara Wilson, Beth Allen, Michael Allen, Jeff Ashworth, Chris Ayers, Ryan Barbare, Brad Barnes, Blake Cheek, Abby Cook, Becky Lane, Justin Matley, Ryan McCammon, Christine Ogletree, Anthony Roach, Carrie Todd, Stephen Vaughn, Jeffrey Crouch, Lisa Macri, and Jesse Caseldine.

# The Original Recipe

## Michael Dorris

Don't ask me to explain — call it making the punishment fit the crime — but I wake up one morning a teenage slave-for-a-day to Kentucky Fried Chicken in Havre, Montana. Mr. VonderHaar greets me at the glass door, his pie-face stern. He wears a white short-sleeve shirt, a tie that stops two buttons above the ledge that his stomach makes over his belt. His too-black hair is combed straight back from his forehead, and he has a widow's peak, like that kid on *The Munsters*.

"I hope you wore comfortable shoes, young lady," he warns.

We both look at my feet. Boots.

He hands me a uniform — a white shift dress and a matching red cap — and points to the ladies'. "You can change in there. I'll lock your clothes in my office for safekeeping."

I snag on the word "lock." The old Sam Cook song from one of Mom's 45's pops into my head. *Uh. Ah. That's the sound of a man, working on the chain gang.*

"What do I do?"

"Tiffany will show you the ropes." And there — bam! — is Tiffany. On her, the uniform looks good. She can even afford

1

to leave the top button carelessly open, there's that much of her to advertise. She wears eyeliner, dark lip pencil with a pale plum accent, a necklace with a heart pendant. Her hair looks like blond meringue.

"You're going to love working here," she informs me. Oh no, she's peppy, too. "Every moment is a challenge."

The girl is certifiable, I think. She has overdosed on fast food. But I smile back at her, twinkly as I can manage.

"Oh yes, and this," Mr. VonderHaar remembers, and hands me a green plastic shower cap. "For in the kitchen. We don't want your hair in the potatoes."

I look at the puff of the shower cap. Even pulled up and tightly packed, my hair will not fit inside it. My head will look like a spore, about to burst.

"I believe in clean," Tiffany confides in me.

She does. I watch as she takes a brush and scrubs the underside of one of the built-in tables.

"Ha," she exclaims, satisfied, and pries something loose. "Gum. They do that — can you imagine? Can you conceive of going into another person's home — and this place is like a home, really — and just sticking a wad under someone's"— she waves her hand with the incriminating pink blob while she searches for the most sacred possible object —"television set?"

Food selection, I learn at 10:45, when the doors open to the public, is the great stumbling block at KFC. Customers arrive in packs, push through the doors, and then stall as they stare slack-jawed at the backlit menu above the ordering counter. Each dish is accompanied by a color photograph of itself, sort of an inducement that tempts, "This could be sitting right in front of you in under five minutes!" Unfortunately, though, the visual aids seem to confuse people at least as much as they help them. Whole hungry families simply can't decide among the major choices presented them. Light meat or dark? Regular or extra crispy? The buffet or à la carte? You can see from the expressions on their faces that they want it all. While they are trying to set their priorities — the thoughts flitting through their brains: *Today a sandwich, tomorrow night a bucket* — more diners arrive and a crowd backs up, jostling unhappily. You'd think that while they were forced to wait, the ones behind would spend their time making up their minds, but no. As each new wave of families or businessmen emerges at the head of the line, they are as perplexed as the ones were who finally just ordered. I stand by the cash register and amuse myself by figuring out what people want before they do. Once I discover that I'm almost always correct, I have to fight the urge to grab a man by the lapels and say, "Don't fight it. You're going to wind up with extra crispy." Or whisper into the ear of a woman, just off a ranch and in town for a shopping spree, "You don't really want a salad, do you?"

My job does not engage the full potential of my brain. In fact, my duties directly contradict a chapter in my tenth-grade science book about the impulse for mastery that drives human evolution. I am in charge of watching the wire baskets that hold the various kinds of chicken and am supposed to alert the cook when a supply gets low so that he can pop another box of pieces into a pressure cooker. The first time I am called upon to do this, I open a little gray eye-level door in the wall that connects to the kitchen and squint through. There's a barrier of warming shelves between me and the stoves, each one holding The Product, as Mr. VonderHaar calls chicken. For a moment I am fascinated by the oddly cut-up shapes KFC favors — breasts, otherwise known as keels, cut along the bias, lumps of meat that could come from almost any part of a bird's anatomy. Could an actual chicken be reassembled from these assorted tidbits? Or would a whole new multi-legged, multi-winged species emerge?

My gaze penetrates past the shelves, and I find myself looking directly into the eyes of the cook — at least I assume that's who it is, because what I see is a man who resembles a giant bunny — white and pink and twitchy.

"What?" the bunny asks.

"Honey-glazed," I reply.

The bunny nods, chuckles to himself, slides a tray of glistening brown blobs off the shelf and through a rectangular slot that opens before me.

"Wow," I breathe softly, but loud enough for Tiffany, who's operating the other register, to hear.

"Derek," she says. "Don't rile him."

It's not a warning I need to hear twice. I wait for her to go on.

"He's been sick," she explains. "They just let him out. But," she adds on a positive note, "he's real good at his job."

We get through the lunch rush — in Havre if you haven't eaten by one-thirty, you wait till supper — and things quiet down so much that I can hear Derek, still chuckling off and on, beyond the wall. Tiffany goes back to her cleaning. Mr. VonderHaar disappears into his office to do whatever he does in there. I, as Tiffany phrases it, mind the store. The chicken bins are almost empty, but the scent of frying oil lingers, even, it seems to me, increases. I watch idly through the plate glass as traffic passes, pickups and moving vans going east and west along Route 2, a Federal Express van, station wagons, a few people on foot. A car turns into the lot, stops, but no one gets out. Then three doors open at once. Dad appears from the driver's side. Simultaneously, the legs of two women swing stiffly from the front and back of the passenger side and grapple for the ground. Old-lady legs in support hose. One of them has an aluminum cane. He has actually brought his mother — the grandmother from Louisville I have met only once before — and her sister, my aunt Edna, here to see me.

I open my mental science book and try to recall the section on genetics, but all that comes up on my screen are Mendel's peas. My grandmother wears her eyeglasses as a necklace. She's dressed in a two-piece electric blue suit and a silky pink blouse with a huge bow under her chin. The skirt is short for a woman of her age, which I estimate to be about eighty. Her mouth, bright with red lipstick, seems to precede her toward the door of the restaurant. Behind her is a tall, thin woman bent at a slight angle at the waist. She uses a cane for support but looks as though she doesn't need it since both the top and bottom halves of her are held precisely straight. She moves slowly, her stance suggesting one of those paper fans opened to its widest extension. A dark red felt hat squashes down a fringe of gray hair, and her eyes are suspicious, as if the KFC is not quite as it should be, as if it is an innocent front for something worse than it is.

I am so upset, I shout at the wall without thinking. "Will you shut up that laughing?"

*Don't rile him.* The words dance across my consciousness. I am surrounded, have eliminated my one available exit through the back door. Derek only becomes louder. *They just let him out.*

"What's all the yelling about?" Tiffany has been spritzing the display case with Glass Wax. She's listening to the radio with earphones, so the only sound that has penetrated is my voice.

She takes off the headset, which has miraculously not made a dent in her hairdo.

"He keeps laughing," I say, and gesture toward the kitchen. Worry blows across Tiffany's features like a bad smell.

"How long?"

"The whole time." It's easier to think of Derek than to hear the whoosh of the front door opening. I smooth the wrinkles from my uniform, run my tongue over my lips.

"Look who's here!" Dad knows I have seen him. I hate the phony tone of his voice.

I stretch a smile across my face, turn around, confront my long-lost grandmother.

"Hello, Ramona," she says.

"It's Rayona, Marcella," Aunt Edna corrects. She's more concerned about getting my name right than in me.

"That name." My grandmother shakes her head in annoyance. "Who could ever remember it?" She looks as though she just stepped off the set of *The Brady Bunch*.

"Something's burning," Dad notices, and sniffs the air.

He's right. Tiffany is knocking on Mr. VonderHaar's office door. "It's Derek," she calls. "I think he's having another one."

Mr. VonderHaar rushes out and passes us without a word. He disappears into the kitchen, Tiffany close behind. The fried odor is suddenly overpowering.

"Excuse me a sec," I say to my grandmother and great-aunt, and follow. My brain can't quite process what my eyes see: mountains of chicken pieces everywhere — in equal parts crispy and extra, it registers. On the sink. Packed onto the warming shelves. Strewn across sacks of instant potatoes along the wall. I've never seen so much chicken, and in the middle of it all, Derek, laughing, tears rolling down his bunny cheeks, laughing so hard he can hardly breathe, so hard he's crying. No, crying but laughing, too, all mixed up. He's crouched on the floor, and Tiffany is beside him. Derek is big, bald, heavy, and Tiffany is petite, but she's urging him to lean against her, to let himself be cradled in her lap.

"Shhh," she says softly, stroking his forehead. "It's okay." Automatically she reaches in the pocket of her uniform, takes out the sponge she was using, and wipes the spittle away from around Derek's mouth.

"I'll call the hospital," Mr. VonderHaar says, and runs back into the restaurant part. "Keep him calm."

I look behind me, and there is Dad, along with my grandmother and Aunt Edna, all goggle-eyed.

"What are those contraptions?" Aunt Edna asks, and points to the row of pressure cookers that line the back wall. They are all vibrating, their little vent-release caps twirling like miniature batons.

"Does anybody know how to turn those things off?" Tiffany is terrified, but she's pinned to the floor by Derek's body. What do the two of them look like, I ask myself. Oh yeah, that marble statue . . . what's it called? *The Pietà.*

"They're going to blow!" Tiffany screams, waking me up to the fact that this is reality and not some *Saturday Night Live* skit.

I stare at Dad. He stares at me.

"Mother," he says. "Come back outside. Aunt Edna."

But Aunt Edna has other ideas. She comes forward, steps over the pile of Derek and Tiffany, and approaches the shaking pots. She seems to be looking for something behind them, then below. The angle of her body becomes more acute as she bends over and reaches under the counter. Suddenly the bubbling noises begin to slack off, the cookers to calm down. Edna straightens to her original 160 degrees. In her hands she holds a disconnected extension cord with the space for six electrical plug-ins.

We all relax, and I try for a joke while Derek continues to chuckle. Even he sounds more gentle now.

"Well, at least we won't have to cook any chicken for the dinner crowd."

"We most certainly will." Tiffany, the highest-ranking KFC official in the room, is outraged. "That chicken"— she nods to the four cardinal directions. "We have no way of knowing whether or not it was prepared under conditions of quality control." She is reciting something out of the official company manual. Her eyes have a blank glaze, as if she is reading from the inside of her head. "We could lose the franchise."

Mr. VonderHaar is back, nodding his agreement. He turns to Dad. "Could you drive us to the hospital?" he asks, looking at Derek. "He's harmless. He just needs someone to hold him, and that will tie up my arms."

"Sure." Dad is happy to escape. I don't blame him.

By the time Dad and Mr. VonderHaar herd Derek into the car, it's nearly four o'clock. We are approaching the hour of the wolf, that point in every twenty-four-hour cycle when a little pilot light goes on in the stomachs of Montanans and they believe themselves not only ready but entitled as American citizens to eat. When this condition prevails, it is never a good idea to get between them and food, and even as my grandmother, my aunt Edna, Tiffany, and I stand together in the wreckage of the usually spotless KFC stainless-steel kitchen, I can sense, in concentric geographic circles — some as close by as the Huber Tire Emporium next door, some as far distant as the tiny soon-to-be ghost towns of the high plains to the east and west — the pricking of a craving for fried chicken.

When it comes to not getting their chicken when they want

it, need it, no excuse is going to be sufficient. People have been trained in what they deserve to expect, and I imagined them now, like a whole town of *Village of the Damned,* their pupils slot machines that show, instead of clusters of cherries or lemons, little bunches of thighs and drumsticks. Any minute now a similar mob will descend on this very KFC, and they aren't in the mood for cole slaw.

"I love your hair," my grandmother tells Tiffany, who beams back her appreciation. "What do you use?"

"I find that over-the-counter conditioners work just as well as those you purchase in salons," Tiffany answers. "And they're much less expensive."

"But you have to make sure to rinse thoroughly." My grandmother grimaces, as if she has learned this fact from bitter trial and error.

"I always do. Otherwise you get buildup."

"Do you wash every day? I hope not."

Tiffany has no poker face. Her expression is a confession of guilt.

"You'll be bald by fifty," my grandmother predicts breezily. "I never wash my own hair. I have a beauty operator do it."

These women have over the years poured far too many chemicals on their heads — that's the only possible explanation.

"Isn't anybody but me worried?" I demand. "Customers are going to start banging on the doors, and if we can't feed them the chicken Derek cooked, what will we do with them?"

My grandmother and Tiffany have been in deep denial and are suddenly stunned. Aunt Edna, on the other hand, has been thinking.

"You've got more chicken?" she asks.

Tiffany nods, slowly, reserving judgment about any idea that is to follow. "But I don't know how to operate the pressure cookers. I'm afraid of them."

Aunt Edna makes a sour face, shakes her head.

"You've got flour, Crisco, skillets?"

"I guess," Tiffany says. "But I don't know the Colonel's formula, the exact mixture of thirty-nine herbs and spices. They only reveal that to the cook."

"Formula!" Aunt Edna scoffs. Her hands are on her narrow hips, her elbows pointing out like two sides of a Texaco star. "I knew Claudia Sanders, took care of her when she got sick. Tried to talk her out of marrying that man. I sat in her kitchen when her mother taught her how to cook."

"You actually knew the Colonel's wife?" I am totally impressed with this woman. First she saves us from being blown to bits, and now she hobnobs with famous people of the past.

Aunt Edna hears the admiration in my voice and likes it. She gives me a twinge of a smile, the first real acknowledgment of me since she arrived. "Honey," she says, "she was just a human being like you and me."

"You know the secret ingredients?" Tiffany acts as though she has just met Albert Einstein.

"Claudia only had one trick to her flavoring," Aunt Edna announces. We all hang in anticipation, and she draws out the suspense. Finally she breaks the silence.

"Table salt," Aunt Edna says. "Plenty of table salt."

I am unused to meeting somebody I am actually related to and being pleasantly surprised, but there is something about Aunt Edna that gets to me. Role models, that's what school counselors are always pushing me to identify with, but the people they parade out are all women astronauts or tennis players or homemaker-senators. I watch Edna, who has to be in her mid-eighties, has to be, take charge of a Kentucky Fried Chicken restaurant, assign us all duties, put on an apron, and start rinsing chicken parts and patting them dry with paper towels. I can't imagine any of those type-A personalities with strings of college degrees after their names and resumes a mile long being able to pull this off. I mean, it's one thing to study, prepare yourself for a job, and then make a success of it, but it's another to just fall into a hole in your life and then make the best of things. Fifteen minutes ago, Aunt Edna was probably tired from her trip, and now look at her, a whirl of activity in a white cloud of flour. It wasn't as though she liked what she had to do — but it wasn't as though she expected to like it, either. She simply pitched in. What was that about courage? How something wasn't real courage unless it was mixed with fear? Well, in Edna's case, work wasn't real work unless it was scrambled with annoyance, but that didn't take anything away from what she accomplished. You could almost see her complaints rolling around inside her, poking out an elbow here, kicking a foot there, but that's where they stayed: inside.

She sees me staring. "What's the matter with you?" she asks, as if she really wants to know.

"Nothing," I say. "It's just that . . ." I'm embarrassed to say what comes into my head.

"That . . . ?" she prods, without once pausing in her food prep.

"I don't know," I say, then chance it. "That I think I kind of take after you, if that makes any sense."

She looks startled. "No," she says. "You would take after Marcella. She's the closer related one."

We both look at my grandmother, who is still exchanging magazine solutions to common beauty dilemmas with Tiffany as they use ice cream scoops to fill little cardboard cups with mashed potatoes.

"Right," I say, and then Edna surprises me again: She laughs.

"Sweetheart," she says, "sometimes I can't figure out how I'm related to her either, but give her time. She's got a big heart."

"You do, too."

"Honey, I'm just big," she says. "Or I was before I shrunk. I've got one piece of advice for you. Don't get old. Now start deep-frying this chicken while I go outside and see if anybody's waiting to eat."

Since the pressure cookers are out of commission, we've improvised, using a huge vat that normally contains gravy. Oil is bubbling inside, and I carefully use a slotted spoon to ladle floured bits of breast and thigh into its depths.

Aunt Edna heads out front, and I imagine her alone against a roomful of stomach-growling westerners. This thought horrifies me. She's from the South, where people are polite, where they please and thank-you and write notes to each other on scented stationery. She doesn't know what she's in for. We are cooking only one kind of chicken, and these people are used to variety.

"Turn the pieces when they brown," I call to Tiffany, then take a deep breath and go out to help Edna.

But of course she doesn't need any help.

"Darling"— she's sweet-talking a man bursting out of a black Sturgis Biker Rally T-shirt, with a skull-and-crossbones tattoo on each forearm —"you just *think* you want Cajun because you don't know about the one-night-only special."

The man looks at her as if she's a holograph, Princess Leia in *Star Wars*. His eyes are yellow, bloodshot. He could have just slashed a tire or something.

"And what would that be?"

Aunt Edna has turned into sweetness itself. She's unrecognizable. She reaches over, squeezes the man's hand where it rests in a fist on the counter.

"You just can't wait to know, can you, hon?"

Before my eyes, the man blushes. He looks as if he is having a stroke, that red.

"Well, I'm going to tell you." Aunt Edna lowers her voice, and every person in line, which at the time numbers about twenty, inclines forward to catch her words. "Homemade southern," she purrs. "My own treasured recipe."

"Your own?" The man knows a good thing when he hears it. *Homemade* is one of those expressions that perks up everybody's ears. It dawns on him that he has the opportunity to get more than his money's worth.

"I'll take it," he decides. My eyes sweep the room. Correction: Everybody decides. Unanimous. "They have homemade," a whisper goes forth like a chain letter, snagging unsuspecting customers the second they pull into the parking lot. "*Real homemade.*"

"I knew you would, sugar," Aunt Edna says. "You just didn't have a choice, did you?"

# QWERTYUIOP

## Vivien Alcock

**J**obs don't grow on trees, the principal of the Belmont Secretarial College was fond of saying.

"Be positive," Mrs. Price told her departing students, as she shook them by the hand in turn. "Go out into the world and *win!* I have every confidence in you."

When she came to the last student, however, her confidence suddenly evaporated. She looked at Lucy Beck and sighed.

"Good luck, my dear," she said kindly, but rather in the tone of voice of someone wishing a snowman a happy summer.

Lucy Beck was young and small and mouse-colored, easily overlooked. She had a lonely O level and a typing speed that would make a tortoise laugh.

"Whoever will want to employ me?" she had asked Mrs. Price once, and Mrs. Price had been at a loss to answer.

Lucy wanted a job. More than anyone, more than anything, she wanted a job. She was tired of being poor. She was fed up with macaroni and cheese and baked beans. She was sick of secondhand clothes.

"We are jumble sailors on the rough sea of life," her mother would say.

Lucy loved her mother, but could not help wishing she would sometimes lose her temper. Shout. Scream. Throw saucepans at the spinning, grinning head of Uncle Bert.

*If I get a job, I'm getting out. He's not drinking up my paycheck, that's for sure. If I get a job. . . .* Trouble was that there were hundreds after every vacancy, brighter than Lucy, better qualified than Lucy, wearing strings of O levels round their necks like pearls.

*Who in their right minds will choose me?* Lucy wondered, setting off for her first interview.

So she was astonished to be greeted by Mr. Ross, of Ross and Bannister's, with enormous enthusiasm. She was smiled at, shaken by the hand, given tea and biscuits, and told that her single O level was the very one they had been looking for. Then she was offered the job.

"I hope you will be happy here," Mr. Ross said, showing her out. There was a sudden doubt in his voice, a hint of anxiety behind his smile, but she was too excited to notice.

"I've got the job! I've got the job!" she cried, running into the kitchen at home. "I'm to start on Monday. I'm to be paid on Friday."

Her mother turned to stare at her.

"You never! Fancy that, now! Who'd have thought it!" she said in astonishment.

Lucy was not offended by her mother's surprise. She shared it. They never trusted luck, but looked at it suspiciously, as if at a stranger coming late to their door.

Ross and Bannister's was a small firm, with a factory just outside the town, making cushions and quilts; and an office on High

Street. On Monday morning, at ten to nine, the door to this office was shut and locked.

She was early. She smoothed down her windy hair and waited.

At five past nine an elderly man, with small dark eyes like currants, and a thick icing of white hair, came hobbling up the stairs. He was jingling a bunch of keys.

"Ah," he said, noticing Lucy. "Punctuality is the courtesy of kings — but a hard necessity for new brooms, eh? You *are* the new broom, I suppose? Not an impatient customer waiting to see our new range of sunburst cushions, by any chance?"

"I'm Lucy Beck," she said, adding proudly, "the new secretary."

"Let's hope you stay longer than the other ones," the man said, and unlocked the door. "Come in, come in, Miss Beck. Come into the parlor, said the spider to the fly. I'm Harry Darke, thirty years with Ross and Bannister's, retired with a silver watch, and now come back to haunt the place. Can't keep away, you see." Then he added oddly, half under his breath, "Like someone else I could mention, but won't."

He looked at Lucy, standing shy and awkward, clutching her bag and uncertain what to do. "Poor Miss Beck, you mustn't mind old Harry. Part-time messenger, office boy, tea-maker, mender of fuses. Anything you want, just ask old Harry. Mr. Ross is down at the factory in the morning, but he's left you plenty of work to be getting on with." He pointed to a pile of tapes on the desk. "Letters to be typed, those are. He got behindhand, with the last girl leaving so quick. Left the same day she came. Shot off like a scalded cat!"

"Why?" Lucy asked curiously.

"Hang your coat in the cupboard here," he said, ignoring her question. "Washroom along the passage to the right.

Kitchenette to the left. We share it with Lurke and Dare, House Agents, and Mark Tower, Solicitor. No gossiping over the teapots, mind. Most of the young things go to Tom's Café for lunch. Put this sign on the door when you leave." He handed her a cardboard notice on a looped string, on which was printed: GONE FOR LUNCH, BACK AT TWO. "Now, is there anything else you want to know before I take off?"

"You're going?" Lucy asked, surprised.

"Yes, my girl. I've errands to do. Not frightened of holding the fort on your own, are you?"

"No, but —"

"You can take a telephone message without getting the names muddled, can't you?"

"Yes, of course."

"Nothing else to it, is there? No need to look like a frightened mouse."

"I'm *not!*"

He looked at her for a long moment, with a strange expression on his face, almost as if he were sorry for her.

"You're very young," he said at last.

"I'm seventeen."

"Don't look it. Look as if you should be still at school. This your first job?"

"Yes."

He shook his head slowly, still regarding her with that odd pity.

"It's a shame," he said; then, seeing her puzzled face, added briskly, "Well, I'll be off, then. Mr. Ross will be in this afternoon."

Yet still he stood there, looking at her. Embarrassed, Lucy turned away and took the cover off the typewriter.

"Just one last thing," the old man said. "That's an electric typewriter."

"I'm used to electric typewriters," Lucy said coldly. She was beginning to be annoyed.

"Not this one. This one's . . . different. You mustn't worry," he said gently, "if it goes a little wrong now and again. Just ignore it. Don't bother to retype the letters. Splash on the old correcting fluid. Look, I got you a big bottle. Liquid Paper, the things they invent! And if that runs out, cross out the mistakes with a black pen — see, I've put one in your tray. Nice and thick, it is. That should keep her quiet."

"I don't make mistakes," Lucy said; then honesty compelled her to add, "Well, not very many. I've been trained. I've got a diploma."

"Yes. Yes, my dear, so they all had," he said sadly, and left.

After the first moments of strangeness Lucy was glad to be alone. No one breathing down her neck. She looked round the office with pleasure. Hers.

Sunlight streamed through the window. The curtains shifted a little in the spring breeze. There was a small blue-and-green rug on the floor.

*I'll have daffodils in a blue vase,* Lucy thought. *I can afford flowers now. Or I will be able to, on Friday.*

Better get on with the work. She sat down, switched on the typewriter, inserted paper and carbons, and started the first tape.

"Take a letter to Messrs. Black and Hawkins, Twenty-eight Market Street, Cardington. Dear Sirs . . ." Mr. Ross's voice came clearly and slowly out of the tape deck. Lucy began to type.

She was a touch typist. She did not need to look at the keys. Her fingers kept up their slow, steady rhythm, while her eyes dreamed round the office, out of the window, down into the sunny street.

". . . our new line of sunburst cushions in yellow, orange, and pink," came Mr. Ross's voice.

There was something odd! A sudden wrongness felt by her fingers, a tingling, an icy pricking. . . .

She snatched her fingers away and stared at the typewriter. It hummed back at her innocently. What was wrong? There was something . . . Her glance fell on the incomplete letter.

Dear Sirs,

I am pleased to inform you that QWERTYUIOP and Bannister's have introduced a new QWERTYUIOP of sunburst cushions in QWERTYUIOP, orange and QWERTYUIOP . . .

She stared at it in horrified bewilderment. What had happened? What had she done? Not even on her first day at the Belmont Secretarial College had she made such ridiculous mistakes. Such strange mistakes — QWERTYUIOP, the top line of letters on a typewriter, repeated over and over again! Thank God there had been no one to notice. They'd think she had gone mad.

She must be more careful. Keep her mind on the job, not allow it to wander out of the window into the sunny shopping street below. Putting fresh paper into the typewriter, she began again.

She was tempted to look at the keyboard. . . . "Don't look at the keys! Keep your eyes away!" Mrs. Price was always saying. "No peeping. You'll never make a good typist if you can't do it by touch. Rhythm, it's all rhythm. Play it to music in your head."

So Lucy obediently looked away, and typed to a slow tune in her head, dum diddle dum dee, dum diddle dum dee. . . . Why did her fingers feel funny? Why were goose pimples shivering her flesh? Was the typewriter really humming *in tune?*

She sat back, clasping her hands together, and stared at the letter in the machine. It read:

> Dear Sirs,
>     YOU ARE SITTING IN MY CHAIR to inform you that GO AWAY a new line of WE DO NOT WANT YOU HERE cushions in yellow, SILLY GIRL and pink. QWERTYUIOP.

She could not believe her eyes. She stared at the extraordinary words and trembled.

"Let's hope you stay longer than the other ones," the old man had said.

Tears came into Lucy's eyes. She tore the sheets out of the typewriter and threw them into the wastepaper basket. Then she put in fresh paper and began again. Grimly, in defiance of Mrs. Price's teaching, she kept her eyes fixed on the keyboard.

> Dear Sirs,
>     We are pleased to inform you that Ross and Bannister's have introduced a new line of Sunburst cushions . . .

With a rattle the typewriter took over. She felt the keys hitting her fingers from below, leaping up and down like mad children at playtime. She took her hands away and watched.

. . . YOU CAN'T KEEP ME OUT THAT WAY, the typewriter printed. YOU'LL NEVER BE RID OF ME. NEVER. WHY DON'T YOU GO. NO ONE WANTS YOU HERE. NO ONE LIKES YOU. GO AWAY BEFORE

Then it stopped, its threat uncompleted.

Lucy leapt up, overturning her chair, and ran to the door.

"Left the same day she came," the old man had said. "Shot off like a scalded cat!"

"No!" Lucy shouted.

She left the door and went over to the window, looking down at the bright shops. She thought of jumble sales and baked beans. She thought of pretty new clothes and rump steaks. She might be young and shy and a little slow, but she was not, no, she was *not* a coward!

She went back and sat down in front of the typewriter and glared at it. There it crouched, like a squat, ugly monster, staring at her with its alphabetical eyes.

Lucy typed quickly:

Are you from outer space?

The typewriter rocked, as if with laughter, its keys clicking like badly fitting false teeth.

IDIOT, it wrote.

Who are you? Lucy typed.

MISS BROOME, it answered.

Lucy hesitated. She did not know quite how to reply to this. In the end she typed:

How do you do? I am Miss Beck.

GO AWAY, MISS BECK

Why should I?

I AM SECRETARY HERE, it stated, this time in red letters.

No, you're not! *I* am! Lucy typed angrily.

The machine went mad.

QWERTYUIOP!" / @QWERTYUIOP£—&()*QWERT-YUIOP+! it screamed, shaking and snapping its keys like castanets.

Lucy switched it off. She sat for a long time, staring in front of her, her face stubborn. Then she took the cap off the bottle of correcting fluid.

For an hour she battled with the machine. As fast as

QWERTYUIOPs and unwanted capitals appeared, she attacked with a loaded brush. The white fluid ran down the typing paper like melting ice cream and dripped thickly into the depths of the typewriter.

YOU'RE DROWNING ME, it complained pathetically, and she swiped at the words with her brush.

HELP!

Another swipe.

PLEASE!

But Lucy showed no mercy. The large bottle was half empty when she reached the end of the letter in triumph.

Yours faithfully,

George Ross, she typed, and sat back with a sigh of relief.

The machine began to rattle. Too late, Lucy snatched the completed letter out of the typewriter. Across the bottom of the otherwise faultless page it now said in large, red capitals:

I HATE YOU!

Furiously she painted the words out.

Mr. Ross came to the office at four o'clock. His eyes went to the corner of the desk where Lucy had put the completed letters. If he was surprised to find so modest a number after a day's work, he did not say so, but picked them up.

"Any telephone messages?" he asked.

"On your desk, sir," Lucy said, and went to make him tea.

When she brought it in on a flowered metal tray, she found Mr. Ross signing the last letter, his pen skidding awkwardly over the thick shiny layer of plastic paper. All the letters were heavily damasked with the dried fluid, like starched table napkins. He glanced up at her a little unhappily.

"Did you have trouble with the machine, Miss Beck?" he asked.

"Yes, sir." (She was afraid to say what trouble in case he thought she was mad.)

"It's only just come back from being serviced," he said wearily.

"I'm sorry, sir. It keeps . . . going wrong."

There was a long silence. Then he said with a sigh, "I see. Well, do what you can. If it's no better at the end of the week . . ."

He let the sentence hang in the air, so that she was not certain whether it would be the typewriter or Lucy Beck who would get the chop.

The next morning, Harry Darke raised his eyebrows when he saw Lucy.

"Still here?" he exclaimed. "Well done, my dear. I never thought I'd be seeing you again. You're braver than you look. Fighting back, eh?"

"Yes," said Lucy briefly. She walked past him and went up to the desk. *Her* desk. Then she took out of her carrier bag a small bunch of daffodils and a blue vase.

"Staking your claim, I see," the old man said, regarding her with admiration. "D'you want me to fill that for you?"

"Thanks."

He came back, carrying a tray.

"Thought I might as well make us tea while I was about it," he said. "Here's your vase."

"Thanks."

"I'll be here till one o'clock today," he said, as she arranged her flowers. "Anything you want to know? Any snags come up I can help you with? Light bulbs changed. Fuses mended. New bottles of correcting fluid handed out. . . ."

"Mr. Darke," Lucy said, looking straight into his small, bright eyes, "who is Miss Broome?"

"Wrong question, Miss Beck."

Lucy thought for a moment, then said, "Who *was* Miss Broome?"

He beamed at her approvingly: "You catch on quick, I'll say that for you. In fact, you're not the timid mouse you look, Miss Beck. You're a right little lion. Need to be, if you're going to take on Miss Broome. Tough old devil, she was."

"Tell me about her," Lucy said, as they sat over their tea.

"She was old Mr. Bannister's secretary. Been here forty-three years, girl, woman, and old misery. Sitting there where you're sitting now, her back straight as a ruler, and a chop-your-head-off ruler too! Her stiff old fingers tapping out the letters one by one, with her nose nearly on the keyboard, so shortsighted she'd become by then. None of your touch typing for her! Every letter she stared in the face like it was a criminal and she the judge. You can't wonder she hates you young girls, with your fingers flying over the keys like white butterflies, and your eyes gazing out into the sunshine. They gave her the push, you know."

"After forty-three years?" Lucy said, shocked into sympathy.

"Well, she was past it, wasn't she? Of course they wrapped it up in tissue paper. Gave her a brass clock and shook her hand and waved her good-bye. She didn't want to go. Didn't have anywhere worth going to — a studio apartment, a gas ring. . . . The old bag didn't have any family who'd own her. This place was her home, this job was all she lived for."

Lucy was silent. Her mother had turned Uncle Bert out once, after a row, shouting that she'd had enough of him. Six weeks later, she had asked him to come back. "He looked so lonely, so lost," she had told Lucy. "All by himself in that horrid little room, with the worn linoleum and the curtains all shrunk."

"Sorry for her, are you?" Harry Darke asked, watching her face.

Lucy hardened her heart.

"It's *my* job now," she said. "I need it. She can't have it forever, it's not fair. It's my turn now."

"So it's a fight to the finish, is it, Miss Beck?" he asked, smiling.

"Yes," she said, and unscrewed the cap from the bottle of correcting fluid.

Her mother was working late that night. Lucy, going into the kitchen to get her own supper, was surprised to find the table neatly laid out with ham and salad, apple pie, and a jug of canned milk. Uncle Bert was sitting waiting for her, beaming proudly.

"Thought I'd have your supper ready," he explained, "now that you're a working girl."

"Thanks," she said, but couldn't resist adding nastily, "I don't get paid till Friday, you know. No good trying to borrow money."

He flushed. "You don't think much of me, do you? Who are you to set yourself up as judge and jury? You don't know what it's like . . . not being wanted. A little kindness would help!"

Lucy noticed his hands were shaking. His collapsing face seemed held together in a scarlet net of broken veins. His eyes were miserable.

"Uncle Bert . . . ," she began.

"What?" He looked at her warily.

"I'm sorry. I'm sorry, Uncle Bert."

"I'm sorry, too, Lucy," he said. "I know it's a nuisance, having me here."

"No! No, it isn't! We want you," she said.

They smiled at each other timidly over the kitchen table,

each remembering the little girl and the handsome uncle, who had once flown kites together in Waterlow Park.

Wednesday was Harry Darke's day off. Alone in the office Lucy put a sheet of paper in the typewriter, and typed quickly:
QWERTYUIOP QWERTYUIOP QWERTYUIOP.
The typewriter gave a jerk, as if surprised, and hummed. Lucy typed:

Dear Miss Broome,
Mr. Darke told me you used to be secretary to Mr. Bannister —
I AM, interrupted the typewriter.

Lucy went on,

I am sorry to have to tell you that Mr. Bannister [she hesitated, wondering how to put it] . . . passed on three years ago, at the age of eighty-six —
LIAR! I DON'T BELIEVE YOU!
It is true, Miss Broome. I have seen his grave in the cemetery. It is not far from yours. I went along last night and left you flowers —
! ! ! ! !
I did. Mr. Darke is worried about Mr. Bannister. He does not know how he will manage without you —
HE CAN MANAGE WITHOUT ME ALL RIGHT! said the typewriter bitterly, HE TOLD ME TO GO. BRASS CLOCK, WHAT DID I WANT WITH BRASS CLOCKS! I WANTED MY JOB.
They only asked you to go because they were worried about your health. [Lucy typed quickly.] Mr.

Darke told me Mr. Bannister was always saying how much he missed you —

? ? ?

Truly. He said Mr. Bannister complained none of the new girls were any good. There was no one like you, he said. . . .

The typewriter was silent. Sunlight glittered on its keys, so that they looked wet.

. . . He must miss you. He's probably in an awful muddle up there, mislaying his wings. Losing his harp. He needs someone to look after him. . . .

The machine was silent. Lucy waited, but it said nothing more.

So she typed:

Good-bye, Miss Broome. Best of luck in your new job.

Yours sincerely,

Lucy Beck, Secretary

She folded the finished letter into a paper dart and sent it sailing out of the window. The wind caught it and carried it away.

Mr. Ross is delighted now with his new secretary. Harry Darke says she's champion, and gives her chocolate biscuits with her tea.

"However did you do it?" he asked.

# Hard Sell

### Tim Wynne-Jones

My first job: *TV Guide* salesman. There was this baseball mitt autographed by Hank Aaron, and you could earn it if you signed up a bunch of people to take *TV Guide* for a year. So I wrote away and they sent me the kit: a blue plastic tote bag with the *TV Guide* logo on it and a strap so I could swing it on my shoulder. The bag was filled with brochures, a pamphlet on salesmanship, and subscription forms. There was even a ballpoint pen. It had the *TV Guide* logo on it, too.

I had got as far as the wide front porch of Mrs. Campion, the nicest lady I knew. If I was going to get turned down on my first sale, I wanted it to be as painless as possible. I hadn't actually rung her doorbell yet. I was standing there in front of her big glass door with a severe case of the What ifs.

What if she was sick? What if the doorbell woke her up and she thought it was the doctor and the front door was locked and so she crawled all the way down two flights of stairs with her last gasp of energy? Just so I could sell her a

*TV Guide.* She had looked okay when I saw her out walking Turlough the day before, but you never knew with old people.

What if Turlough had rabies? Turlough was an Irish wolfhound. He could lick your face without jumping up. Small children had been sent to hospital after being thwacked in the stomach by his wagging tail. What if he'd met up with a rabid fox in the park and as the door opened he leapt on me, not remembering I was a friend? What if he'd already eaten Mrs. Campion? She wouldn't need a *TV Guide.*

That morning my dad had said, "What this country needs is more good salesmen." I wasn't so sure anymore.

Suddenly I realized that Turlough was standing on the other side of the glass front door. He looked friendly enough with his mouth lolling open and saliva dripping all over the tiles. But you could never tell with Irish wolfhounds. There was still time to leave and try somewhere else.

But then, before I could move, there was Mrs. Campion. She had seen me and was coming to the door even though I hadn't rung the bell. Maybe I had that special gift that only the best salesmen possess.

"Clarke, how long have you been standing out here? Come in, come in."

Turlough was on me like a shot, licking my face and thwacking me with his tail. He had a big hard blob of a cast on the end of his tail. He had broken it wagging it against a tree or something. This dog was just too happy.

I pushed him away and began my spiel.

"Hi, Mrs. Campion. Actually, I just dropped by to see if you'd be interested in subscribing to *TV Guide.*"

At this point, having taken the casual approach the pamphlet recommended, I deftly opened my blue plastic tote and pulled out the latest copy of the magazine. Unfortunately, I also pulled out about a hundred subscription forms, which fell on the welcome mat. Turlough walked all over them before Mrs. Campion dragged him off.

"You big lunk," she said. Not to me, to the dog. Turlough barked. He always barked when she called him a big lunk. It was sort of a game.

"Well, this might be a very good idea, Clarke," she said, as she looked through *TV Guide*. I was gathering up the pawed-over subscription forms and stuffing them back into my blue plastic tote bag.

"What if you're away at the cottage?" I said. "They come every week, you know. They'll pile up on your front porch and then a thief combing the neighborhood for likely targets will know you're away and break in."

Mrs. Campion had been reading something in *TV Guide*. "Pardon?" she said. Her reading glasses were poised on the end of her nose.

"I was just thinking," I said, stuffing the last of the forms in my tote bag. "You probably don't watch much TV."

"Well," she said. "You're right about that, but that's all the more reason to have something I can look through beforehand. See what there is to look forward to."

I don't know what it is about the What ifs. My mother says I'm plagued by them.

"But you're at the cottage most of the summer," I reminded her. I knew this because I did her lawns and kept an eye on the house.

"That's a good point," said Mrs. Campion. "Maybe I should get two subscriptions: one for here and one for there."

This I hadn't counted on. Two subscriptions at one house! What if that happened all the way up Clemow Avenue, all over the neighborhood, all over the city! They'd have to send me a mitt and a bat and a uniform. And if things kept up that way, soon they'd have to send me Hank Aaron himself. I'd be the owner of the Milwaukee Braves (that was the name of their team in those days), and it would have all started on a summer morning on Mrs. Campion's front step.

I became aware, suddenly, of Turlough nibbling with his huge yellow Irish wolfhound teeth at the corner of my blue plastic tote bag with the *TV Guide* logo on it.

"You big lunk," I said. Turlough barked. I looked up and Mrs. Campion wasn't there. Dimly I recalled her saying, "Just a minute," because dimly I recalled that the telephone had rung. Sometimes when I'm having an attack of the What ifs, things get pretty dim. It gets like *The Twilight Zone*.

I felt stupid. She probably had said, "I'll be right back, Clarke," in her nicest voice. And there I was staring off into space like the very last of the dodo birds about to walk on his short stout legs into a camp of dodo-bird hunters.

"You big lunk," I said to Turlough, scratching him behind the ear.

"Woof," he said.

Mrs. Campion was still on the phone. Or maybe she was just politely waiting until I left so that she didn't have to disappoint me. She was just being nice about buying two subscriptions. They were always so generous about paying me for doing the lawn and other errands.

Suddenly it seemed completely crummy that these nice neighbors should be plagued by me trying to sell them stuff. I could imagine Mr. Campion at dinner. "What's he selling now, dear, a new Pontiac? Of course, we'll buy it. Clarke's such a nice kid. . . ."

I couldn't stand it. I didn't want her to buy *TV Guide* just to be nice. I went all-over cold. If she really wanted it, she would already have a subscription, a smart woman like Mrs. Campion. Why hadn't I thought of that before?

I couldn't stand the suspense any longer. I had to get out of there — I had to act quick. I pushed Turlough backward into the vestibule.

"Tell her I had to go home for lunch," I whispered to him.

"Woof," he said. Maybe "lunch" sounded like "lunk" to him.

Then I was gone. I ran down the street as fast as I could. I was already home when I realized that I had left my one and only copy of *TV Guide* with Mrs. Campion. With a kind of sad relief, I realized that my career as a door-to-door salesman was over.

My mother was at the door when I arrived.

"Mrs. Campion just phoned to apologize for being so rude," she said. "She had to talk to Mrs. Henkell-Trocken about some urgent March of Dimes business."

"She wasn't rude," I said, slumping in the chair in the hall, out of breath.

"She wants two subscriptions to *TV Guide*," said Mom. "And Mrs. Henkell-Trocken is interested, too."

"Oh, that's just great!" I said. And stomped up to my room.

Apart from the baseball mitt with Hank Aaron's signature, one of the reasons I had wanted to sell *TV Guide* was because that summer was boring. We didn't have a cottage, and my parents couldn't afford to send me to camp, and Cary and Tony and the other guys were all away. But selling was too difficult. I knew that now. For someone plagued with the What ifs, it was a minefield. It was like asking a person on crutches to cross a floor covered with banana peels. It was like asking Godzilla to sell bone china at Birks Jewelers.

It was like asking a blind person to interior-decorate your home.

After lunch, I told Mom I was going to go and see Mrs. Campion, but when I hopped on my bike, I rode straight over to Cary's and then to Tony's, even though I knew they were away. I was hoping maybe one of them had caught chicken pox and had been sent home. Then I'd catch chicken pox. Catching chicken pox wouldn't be so bad. Scratching would at least give me something to do.

But neither of them was there. So I rode over to the park.

It was noonday hot. I pulled to a stop in the shade of a huge chestnut tree and surveyed the grounds. There were some kids there, but no one I knew.

At one end of the park, five guys were playing weird games with a girl's bicycle. One of them was sitting in the basket on the front. I didn't think I wanted to know them.

I looked back toward the Lyon Street stairs. Mrs. Campion! She was out walking Turlough. She'd see me if I tried to make a run for it. All I could do was slink over to the bushes — there were openings and paths there — and hope she didn't notice my bike, which I left on the grass under the tree. One wheel turning.

The bushes were deep and dry and thirsty with yellow flowers. I parted the dusty leaves and trained my eye on Mrs. Campion. As soon as she passed, I planned to sneak back out and head up the Lyon Street exit. By now she probably had signed up fifty people to buy *TV Guide* from me. Anyway, I was so busy watching her progress that I didn't notice the girl sitting quietly a little bit up the hill behind me. Not until she spoke.

"Who are you hiding from, please?" she asked.

I turned. She was about seven, I guess. Her skin was chestnut brown, her hair blue-black. She wore a yellow ribbon in it and a clean yellow dress and yellow sneakers. She didn't look like she usually hung out in the bushes.

"I am sorry," she said. "I astonished you."

"It's okay," I said. But I was pretty astonished.

She smiled and slid on her backside down the hill next to me. "Is it those horrid boys who you are hiding from?" she asked.

I didn't answer right off. I was staring at the red mark on her forehead. It was perfectly round, like a bullet hole. I had never seen someone from India before, not up close. Or maybe I had, in a magazine, but never a real kid.

"Those reckless boys have stolen my bicycle," she said.

I looked out across the park through the dusty leaves and the veil of yellow flowers to where the boys were. They were standing in a wide circle playing a kind of catch with the girl's bike, shooting it back and forth to one another. They looked tough. Probably went to Glashan Elementary.

"You should get it back," I said. Luckily, the little girl didn't seem to notice what a stupid remark it was.

"I told them I was going home immediately to get my big brother, who would show them a thing or two," she said.

"But he wasn't home?"

"I don't have a big brother," she said sadly. Then her eyes grew huge and she smiled. "But very soon I will have a little brother."

I looked back at the boys across the park. "How soon?" I said. I didn't think he would be much help.

"Why, this very afternoon," she said. "My mother is going into the hospital and she will come back with a baby and I am hoping — oh, I am hoping — it will be a brother. It is because of him that I have this new bicycle."

I couldn't get over it. It was a brand-new bike and she was as cheery as could be even though it had been stolen. I wished I could do something. I didn't think they would really take it away with them. Maybe they'd dump it in the fountain or something and I could help the girl fish it out. If only I could assure her that that was all that would happen.

"Perhaps you know these boys," she said. "And could ask them for my bicycle back?"

I tried to imagine it. "Hi, guys. Mind if I take this bike back? Thanks." I had a pretty good imagination, but I couldn't see it happening like that.

"You are big, too," she said hopefully. Then she looked serious again. "Well, almost big."

Maybe when they get good and bored, I thought, they'll leave it. And if they don't? Then I would ask for it. But if I did, even if they gave it to me — which I doubted — they would remember me and probably get me some other time. Or *my* bike. I would be marked for life.

"They called me a wog," she said. "Do you know, please, what that might be?"

"Shhh!" I said. Mrs. Campion and Turlough were walking nearby on the path. Turlough sniffed my bike. Mrs. Campion dragged him away. She was afraid he was going to pee on it, but he knew whose bike it was even if his master didn't.

A wog. I didn't know what it was, but it made my blood boil. My eyes wouldn't focus properly. That's when I noticed that the big floppy yellow flowers behind which I was hiding were infested with little black bugs.

"Turlough," said Mrs. Campion, yanking on his leash. "You big lunk."

Turlough barked.

That's when it came to me.

"I could be your brother," I whispered.

The girl gazed at me with an amused look in her eye. "You have yellow hair," she said.

But I was miles ahead of her. "Come on," I said. I grabbed her hand and sprang out of the bushes, much to Mrs. Campion's surprise.

"Why, Clarke," she said, her hand on her chest. "You scared us, didn't he, Turlough?"

Turlough woofed the deep-in-the-throat-I'm-a-wolf-hunting-dog kind of bark he always did. It was great to hear.

"Can I borrow him?" I asked.

"Borrow Turlough?"

"Just for a minute," I said. Then I explained about the guys who had stolen the girl's bike and how they'd called her a wog. Mrs. Campion was shocked.

"And what is your name, my dear?" she said.

"Amila," said the girl, shaking Mrs. Campion's hand.

So Mrs. Campion sat down on the nearest park bench with Amila while I went about my plan.

Turlough and I nosed around in my bike bag. There was my baseball mitt — my scruffy old falling-apart mitt that I would now be stuck with for life — my Milwaukee Braves cap and my mirror sunglasses. Even though every kid I knew was away somewhere, I always carried my baseball stuff just in case I ran into a game. Now it seemed I was going to get a completely different kind of game.

My yellow hair was summer-short. Although the hat didn't completely cover it, it was a start. There was also my bike repair kit. I never went anywhere without it. In it was a can of oil. I "goinked" some on my fingers. That's the sound the can makes — *goink, goink, goink.*

I spread the oil on the back of my hand. My hand got brown. Not very brown, like Amila. Just a kind of smeary, oily brown.

Carefully, with my eyes scrinched shut, I started applying the oil to my face and neck and arms. *Goink, goink, goink.*

I pushed Turlough away. He was trying to lick my face. I goinked some oil on his nose to keep him at bay.

"Ah!" said Amila when she saw me. "Now you really are turning into my big brother." But she was teasing me. I wasn't anywhere near as brown as she was. I just smelled funny.

"What are you doing?" asked Mrs. Campion.

"It's just a little something to hide behind," I said. "Come on, Turlough."

Holding his lead with both hands close to his thick neck, I set off. We headed across the grass to the circle of boys playing catch with Amila's new bike.

I didn't know what it would be like to be blind, but I tried to imagine it. I kept my eyes open behind my mirror glasses, but I walked as if I was being led by Turlough. And I let Turlough lead me right into the middle of the circle game. Just as one of the boys launched the bike.

"Hey, watch out!"

The bike came straight toward me. Blindly, I put out my hand, stopping it before it could hit me. It fell at my feet. One boy ran to get the bike, but with all the excitement, Turlough barked, and the boy stopped.

"You could get killed," he said.

"Oh, I'm sorry," I said, trying to imitate Amila's voice. "You astonished me." I stopped right there in the middle of the circle and blindly patted Turlough's big head with my free hand.

None of the boys came toward me.

"So get lost!" said one of them.

"Actually, I am lost," I said. "My little sister told me some boys had stolen her bicycle and I am looking for them to teach them a lesson. Could you, please, direct me to these horrid boys?"

One of them moved a little closer. "Get outa here," he said. "We'll give you to ten, 'cause you're a blind wog."

I leaned close to Turlough's ear. "Big lunk," I whispered.

"Woof," said Turlough.

The nearest boy backed up.

I hadn't known exactly what I was going to do. I just figured that with Turlough there, it really didn't matter what I did. Now it was coming to me.

"What is that, Turlough?" I said.

I leaned close again as if trying to hear something. Close enough to whisper the *L* word whenever I felt like it.

"You say these are the horrid boys? (Lunk.)"

"Woof."

"There are how many? (Lunk.)"

"Woof."

"Five? (Lunk.)"

"Woof."

"So many boys ganging up on a little girl? (Lunk.)"

"Woof."

The boys weren't holding back anymore. They were moving in. Pressing closer. I hadn't counted on that. Maybe they wanted to hear what I was whispering to the dog. Or maybe they were beginning to realize what just about everybody does a few minutes after they meet Turlough. He may be very large, but his face is so friendly, you know he couldn't hurt a fly. Not on purpose, at least.

"That dog ain't talking."

"And that kid ain't blind."

"And he ain't a wog, either. He's a fake."

I had to think quick. They were closing in, talking each other up, getting braver. I held Turlough close. He was panting away and smiling. I knew what *he* was thinking. "Oh, boy. Company."

Soon they were crowding all around me.

One of them reached out across the dog and slid a finger across my cheek. He looked at the grease, smelled it.

"What is this?" he said.

I gulped for breath. When I spoke, I dropped the fake accent.

"It's wog juice," I said. "I'm part white, part *wog*."

"Hey, Ernie, looks like you got some on you," said one of the guys. They laughed as Ernie wiped the bicycle oil off on his jeans.

"Shut up," he said, shoving one of the guys.

"Ernie's a wo-og," they chanted. "Ernie's a wo-og."

"Yuck," said one of them. "And he stinks like a wog, too."

That did it. I moved in close to the one nearest me. He backed off, maybe only because my face stank of bicycle oil.

"When the sun gets really hot, it brings out the wog in me," I yelled at his face. "And the part of me that's wog is really angry about what you did to this brand-new bicycle! Look at it."

They looked. I couldn't believe it.

I reached down, grabbed the bike by the handle and jerked it up. I was breathing hard. The basket on the front was stretched out of shape. My throat and face ached. I was afraid I was going to cry. I couldn't talk to them anymore. Couldn't look at them.

"Look at this, Turlough," I shouted. "Look what these big lunks have done."

Turlough barked. Angrily.

The boys really started backing off now. Turlough was dancing around, pulling on his leash.

"We were just playin' around," said one.

"You can have the dumb bike," said another.

"Come on, guys," said a third.

And then they were off. Like fly-hunting bats in the twilight, zigzagging every which way, they dipped and darted toward the Lyon Street exit.

Mrs. Campion and Turlough and I walked Amila and her bike home.

"That was very brave, Clarke," said Mrs. Campion.

When I told my mother about the incident in the park, she said, "And did you remember to talk to Mrs. Campion about the *TV Guide* subscription?"

I hadn't. It had completely slipped my mind. Funny how you can forget important things like *TV Guide* when you are rescuing a little girl's brand-new bike from five thugs. I didn't say that to my mom. I said something I'd heard my dad say.

"No. Some of us just aren't cut out for sales, Mom."

I guess Amila found out my address from Mrs. Campion. Anyway, that evening just before dinner, she arrived at my house. I went to the door. She was taking a cloth bundle from the wrecked basket of her bike.

"For you and your family," she said, handing it to me. The bundle was warm in my hands.

My mom came to the door and introduced herself. I opened the bundle. Fragrant steam came out as the flaps of warm, white cloth fell open.

"They are called *samosas*," Amila said. "You eat them."

I didn't know what to do, so she showed me. She ate one of the little savory packets — kind of like a semicircular egg roll. I tried one. And so did my mother. Then my father came out with his newspaper to see what all the noise was about and he tried one, too. There we all were munching *samosas*. They were very spicy.

"My auntie made them," said Amila. Then her eyes got very

big. "But I have forgotten the most important news, Clarke. Now I am the proud sister of *two* brothers."

"Twins?" I said.

"No," she said. Laughing, she ran down the path to her new bicycle and, pumping hard, headed home.

# A Job for Valentín

## Judith Ortiz Cofer

I can't swim very well, mainly because my eyesight is so bad that the minute I take off my glasses to get in the pool, everything becomes a blob of color and I freeze. But I managed to talk my way into a summer job at the city pool anyway, selling food, not being a lifeguard or anything. It's where I want to be so I can be with some of my friends from school who don't have to work in the summer. I'm a scholarship student at Saint Mary's, and one of the few Puerto Ricans in the school. Most of the other students come from families with more money than us. Most of the time that doesn't bother me, but to have some nice clothes and go places with my school friends, I have to work all year — as a supermarket cashier mostly, until now. I got the job with the Park Services because my friend Anne Carey's father is the park director. All I'll be doing is selling drinks and snacks, and I get to talk to everyone since the little concession stand faces the Olympic-size pool and the cute lifeguard, Bob Dylan Kalinowski. His mother is a sixties person and she named him after the old singer from that time. Bob Dylan lettered in just about everything this year.

As I walk to the bus stop, I'm thinking about how good it's going to be to get away from El Building this summer. It does take me forty-five minutes to get to the other side of town where the pool is, but it's worth it. It's a good first day. The woman, Mrs. O'Brien, who shows me around, says I don't need any training. I can run a cash register, I can take inventory, and I am very friendly with customers — even the obnoxious ones. The only thing I don't really like is that Mrs. O'Brien tells me that she expects to be told if I ever see Bob Dylan messing around on the job.

"People's lives, *children's* lives, are in that young man's hands," she says, looking toward the lifeguard stand where Bob Dylan is balancing himself like a tightrope walker on the edge for the benefit of Clarissa Miller, who is looking up at him like she wants him to jump down into her arms. She's about six foot tall and well muscled herself, so I get distracted thinking how funny it would be to see her tossing him over her shoulder and taking him home, like she's always saying she wants to do. Mrs. O'Brien brings me back when she says in an insistent voice, "Keep an eye on him, Teresa, and use that phone there to call me, if you need to. I'm in my office most of the time." (She's Mr. Carey's assistant, or something, and her office is luckily kind of far from the pool and store.)

I say, "Yes, ma'am," even though I feel funny about being asked to spy on Bob Dylan. He's a senior at my school, a diver for the varsity swim team, and, yeah, a crazy man sometimes. But if they gave him the job as a lifeguard, they ought to trust him to do it right, although the fact that Anne Carey is absolutely and hopelessly in love with him probably had something to do with his getting the job.

That was the first day. Except for O'Brien asking me to fink on Bob Dylan, I had a good time taking in the action at poolside. And one thing nobody knows: I'm interested in Bob

Dylan too. But I would never hurt Anne. And as of now, he is playing the field, anyway. He flirts with every girl in school. Even me. That's what I really like about Bob Dylan — he's democratic. But not too humble: I once heard him say that God had given him a great body and it was his duty to share it.

The second day is bad news. A disaster. I got assigned a "mentally challenged" assistant by the city. There's a new program to put retarded people to work at simple jobs so they can make some money, learn a skill, or something. I thought I approved of it when the man came to Saint Mary's to explain why these "mildly handicapped" individuals would be showing up around the school, doing jobs like serving lunch and picking up around the yard. At first they got hassled a little by the school jerks, but Sister sergeant-at-arms Mary Angelica started flashing suspension slips at us, and then everybody soon got used to the woman who smiled like a little girl as she scooped up mashed potatoes and made what she called snow mountains on our plates. And we learned not to stare at the really cute guy who stared right through you when he came in to empty the wastebaskets in our classrooms. I sometimes wondered what he thought about. Maybe nothing. This guy could have been on TV except when you looked into his eyes: they were like a baby's eyes, sort of innocent, but sad too. Nobody believed it when the rumor started that he wasn't born like that, but had been a war hero in Vietnam, where he got shot in the head. Who knows? I didn't think he was that old.

The thing is, I don't have anything against these handicapped people, but I don't want to spend my whole summer with one. Stuck in a tiny space. And really, there's nothing for one of them to do here. Besides, how is it going to look to Bob Dylan and my other friends? They're not going to want to hang around the store with someone like that around. Let's face it, that VACANCY sign on their faces gets to you after a while.

But there he is. My new *partner* is being led in by Mrs. O'Brien. I am watching them walk very slowly from her office, across the playground, and toward my store. She called me a few minutes ago to tell me that Mr. Carey has decided that it would be a wonderful opportunity to place Valentín as my assistant in the store. He is Puerto Rican like me, thirty years old, and mildly challenged. He has the IQ of a third grader, she tells me. A *bright* third grader. And he is an artist. I can't help but wonder what others are going to say about this guy. It's hard enough to get people to believe that you have normal intelligence when you're Puerto Rican, and my "assistant" will be a living proof for the prejudiced.

"He's brought some of his creations," Mrs. O'Brien told me in a cheerful voice. "We're letting him sell them at the store."

"You're letting him sell his crayon drawings at the store?" I couldn't believe my ears. If this woman had deliberately tried to humiliate me, she couldn't have thought of a better way to do it.

"They are not crayon drawings, Teresa," she said, a little less cheerfully. "I told you Valentín is gifted in art. . . . Well, you'll see in a few minutes." Then she hung up and I watched them coming.

Old Valentín has the posture of a gorilla. And so much hair on his head and his arms, and overflowing his shirt collar, that my first impression is that he should be put to work in a cooler place. I mean, he is furry. And he's carrying a huge shopping bag that seems to drag him down. Great. Wonderful. I glance over at Bob Dylan, and I see that he is spying on me through his binoculars. Under other circumstances I'd be enjoying it. At the moment I feel like quitting the job. My mother tried to talk me out of taking this job because it's so far from home and she thinks I'm going to fall in the pool and drown or something. Now I wish I'd taken her advice.

Mrs. O'Brien steps up into the store and sort of takes Valentín's hand and guides him in. But then she is distracted by yelling and running at poolside. No running is allowed. Bob Dylan is supposed to blow his whistle when the little kids do it. But he is nowhere in sight. Mrs. O'Brien takes off for the pool without another word, and I'm left facing Valentín. He's standing there like a big hairy child waiting to be told what to do.

"I'm Terry," I say. Nothing. He doesn't even look up. This is going to be even worse than I thought.

"What's your name?" I say it real slow and loud. Maybe he's a little hard of hearing.

"*Soy* Valentín," he says in Spanish. His deep voice surprises me. Then he hands me the big shopping bag. I try to take it, but it's really heavy. He takes it back very gently and lifts it onto the counter. Then he starts taking out these little animals. They are strange-looking things, all tan in color and made from what I first think is string. But when I pick one up, it feels like rubbery skin. They are made from rubber bands. Valentín takes them out one at a time: a giraffe, a teddy bear, an elephant, a dog, a fish, all kinds of animals. They are really kind of cute. The elephant and the fish are about three inches tall and both chubby.

"Is it a whale?" I pick the fish thing up, and Valentín takes a long look at it before answering.

"*Sí*," he says.

"Do you speak English?" I ask him. I can speak Spanish, but not that good.

"*Sí*," Valentín says.

He arranges his rubber-band menagerie on one side of the counter, taking a long time to decide what goes next to what for some reason. Mrs. O'Brien walks in looking very upset.

"Teresa, does he do this often?"

I know she's talking about Bob Dylan clowning around on the job and taking off to talk to people sometimes.

"This is only my second day here," I protest. And maybe my last, I think.

"Teresa, someone could drown while that boy is away from his post."

I don't say anything. I was not hired to spy on Bob Dylan. Although I do plan to keep my eyes on him a lot for my own reasons. He's fun to watch.

"We'll discuss this again later." Mrs. O'Brien turns to Valentín, who is still taking animals out of the bag and lining them up on the counter. He must have brought a hundred of them.

"I see you two have met. Teresa, it is Valentín's goal to sell his art and make enough money to buy himself a bicycle. He lives in a group home on Green Street and he wants to have transportation so that he can get a job in town. I think it's a wonderful idea, don't you?"

I'm saved from having to answer by Valentín, who is handing me a handful of price tags. They all say $2.00.

"He wants you to help him price his art, Teresa." No kidding, I think. Mrs. O'Brien is acting like she thinks I'm as slow as her newest employee here. She sighs, looking out at the pool again. Bob Dylan is back in his lifeguard chair. His whistle is going full blast, and his arms are waving wildly as he directs people in the pool to do this and that. She and I both know that he's making fun of her, putting on a show for a girl's benefit, or maybe mine. I try not to smile. He looks so good out there.

Mrs. O'Brien says again, "Teresa, if anything goes wrong, use that phone there to call me. At five I'll come get Valentín. See if you can get your friends to buy his art. It's for a worthy cause!"

Valentín watches her leave the store with the look of a child left at school for the first time. It's so strange to see an adult acting like he's lost and maybe about to cry. His face shows every emotion he feels. As Mrs. O'Brien leaves, he looks anxious. His hands are trembling a little as he continues to line up his little rubber-band zoo on top of the counter. I decide to go ahead and put the price tags on them, since I'm not doing anything else. Each tag is like a little collar, and I put them around the necks of the creatures. They feel oddly like living things. I guess the rubber is like skin and takes in the heat from the sun. I press the teddy bear down, and it bounces off the counter. Valentín catches it like a ball and puts it back precisely where it had been. He is frowning in concentration as he once more checks to see if anything has moved since two minutes ago when he last looked. It's beginning to get on my nerves. His lips are moving, but nothing is coming out.

"Please speak louder, Valentín. I can't hear you." I have put a $2.00 tag on each rubber-band beast, even though one big sign would have done the job just as well. I turn to face him, and he points to his shopping bag.

"You have more *art* in there?" I hear the sarcasm creeping into my voice, but I am not here to baby-sit a retarded man who has a thing for rubber bands. Soon Clarissa, Anne, and my other friends will be here, and I'd like to talk to them in private.

Valentín moves around me cautiously toward his bag. He acts like he's afraid I'm going to bite his head off. It's really annoying. I get out of his way — as I said, the place is very small — and he takes the bag and goes to sit in the folding chair near the soft-drink machine. He pulls out a big box with his name printed in huge letters in different color markers. He opens the lid and sticks his hand in. He shows me a bunch of thick rubber bands like fat worms. He smiles.

"*Trabajo*," he says. Work. It is his job.

"Yes. Make more *animales*," I say. That will keep him busy and out of my way. I watch him wind a rubber band around his index finger into a tight little ball. He attaches the ball to a frame he shapes out of very thin wire. He does it so slowly and carefully that it makes me want to scream. A real animal could evolve from a single cell in the time it takes Valentín to make the first quarter inch of one of his creations. I am so distracted watching him that Bob Dylan's deep voice startles me.

"Hey, is that your new Puerto Rican boyfriend there, Terry? I thought you were my girl." He is pulling himself up onto the counter by pushing up with his hands. The muscles on his arms are awesome. He's all shiny because he's rubbed oil on his body, and his long brown hair is wet. He looks like Mr. July on my hunk-of-the-month calendar.

"Hi." I cannot think of anything else to say because what I am thinking is not suitable material for a family park. This is what I took this job for — the view.

"Give me an o.j. on the rocks, little mama. And introduce me to el hombre over there. And what are these . . . ?" Bob Dylan always talks like a combination of TV jock and radio announcer from 1968. It's his parents' influence. They lived in a commune when they were hippies, and even now they sign Christmas cards with a peace sign. They also grow their own food in their homemade greenhouse. People at school say that it's the mushrooms in the basement that make Bob Dylan and his family such happy campers. The Kalinowski adults wear ponchos in the winter and tie-dyed T-shirts with embroidered jeans in the summer. Bob Dylan is like them in his personality, but he has to wear a suit and tie at Saint Mary's. With his body he looks like Clark Kent about to flex his chest and let that big *S* burst through.

"This is Valentín." I point to him, and Valentín quickly ducks his head like someone's going to punish him. His rubber-band ball is about a half inch in diameter now. "He makes them to sell. To buy himself a bicycle."

Bob Dylan picks up the fish and brings it up to his face. He makes his eyes cross as he looks at it. I have to laugh.

Valentín stops what he's doing to stare at us. He looks afraid. But he doesn't move. I take the fish back and put it in its place on the counter.

"VERY NICE, MY MAN!" Bob Dylan says, too loud. Valentín drops the little ball, and it bounces and rolls under the counter. I can tell that he's upset as he gets on all fours to go after it.

Bob Dylan laughs and jumps down from the counter and kisses my hand all in one motion.

"My Chiquita banana," he says, "stay true to me. Don't give my whereabouts out to the enemy. I shall return."

"Bye," I say. I am such a great conversationalist, inside my own head. Really, I say brilliant things all the time. It's just that nobody hears them.

I hand the can of orange juice and a cup of ice to Bob Dylan. He struggles to dig some coins out of his black Speedo trunks, which seem to be spray-painted on. Art is one of my best subjects, and I stand back and admire the simple, tasteful design of the trunks.

"Thanks," I say when the quarters pop out of his pocket, continuing to show off my amazing vocabulary.

"You are always welcome. Tell me the Spanish word for always."

"*Siempre.*"

"Siempre," Bob Dylan repeats. But he's already looking away. We have both heard familiar giggles. It's Clarissa and Anne, one tall and one short blond in their skimpy bathing suits. I see his eyes go from one to the other. More than one girl at a time is difficult for Bob Dylan. He specializes in the one-to-one approach. Lock eyes with her, say a line from one of Mrs. Kalinowski's old sixties records, something like "Light My Fire." And that's all it takes. That's all it takes with me, anyway. I see him veer off in the direction of his lifeguard stand while waving to them, letting them get a view of his entire, glorious self. He will let them come to him separately: divide and conquer. He looks over his shoulder at me and winks, covering all the bases.

I hear a sort of grunt and jump away from the counter. It's just Valentín, who has finally retrieved his rubber ball out from behind some cartons and is struggling to get back on his feet. He looks a little embarrassed, and I guess that he's really been hiding. This isn't going to work. I haven't decided whether I'm going to keep this job, but I do have a responsibility to train this guy while I'm here.

"Valentín, let me show you how to pour drinks. You see those two girls coming this way? They'll order a root beer and a diet cola. I'll do the cola and then you do the root beer. Watch."

He watches me very closely, following my hands with his eyes like someone playing chess or something. Clarissa and Anne are at the counter, so I nod at him to pour the root beer.

"Hey, Terry. How's the job going?" Clarissa booms out. She's not only the tallest and strongest girl at Saint Mary's but also the loudest. I hear a crash behind me and turn around to see that Valentín has dropped the cup of ice all over everything. Clarissa startled him. He's really a case. The most nervous human being I've ever seen. He just stands there with a look of such shock on his face that both my friends start giggling. Valentín's expression changes, and I see that he's turning red from his neck up. Embarrassed. He is so easy to figure. I'd hate to have a face that showed the whole world what I think all the time.

Then he starts all over again, filling new cups with ice and pouring the drinks so slowly and carefully that Clarissa pretends to be snoring and Anne starts playing with the rubberband animals, making the giraffe fight with the horse. When Valentín brings the drinks to them, his hands are trembling. I can see that he's really having to concentrate not to spill the drinks on the counter, especially since his eyes are glued to the empty spots where the giraffe and horse are supposed to be. I hand the drinks to my friends.

"This is Valentín," I say, not smiling, to try to let them know not to upset him by laughing, even though his constantly changing facial expressions are really funny. "He's helping me out, and he's selling these so that he can buy himself a bicycle."

"You make them yourself, right?" Anne is trying to be nice — I can see that. And she should be; after all, it's her father who hired Valentín. But she's still fooling around with his animals, making them slide across the counter and messing up the perfectly straight row that Valentín made with them.

"*Dos dólares,*" Valentín says to Anne, and extends one of his hairy hands out.

"He says they are two dollars each," I translate for Anne, and raise one eyebrow to try to communicate that she'd better either buy or put back the merchandise, or he may just stand there watching her hands all day.

"I know that much Puerto Rican, I mean Spanish, gracias very much, Terry." Anne puts the horse back in line and sticks the giraffe into the top of her bathing suit. She hands me a five-dollar bill. Valentín watches every move, following me to the cash register while I make change. I hand him two one-dollar bills. He inspects them and puts them into his shirt pocket, which he then buttons. He smiles at me. Then he goes to the back and starts to pick up the ice cubes he dropped, one by one.

When I turn back to my friends, they are both grinning. The giraffe is peeking out of Anne's top, which makes me laugh.

"Well, Teresa, we were just saying that we think you're going to have a *very interesting* work experience this summer," Clarissa says, looking pointedly in Valentín's direction.

We talk for a while, mainly about Bob Dylan, who has been looking at us through his binoculars. Anne is pointing to her giraffe so that he will zoom in on it. Soon I get a crowd of kids asking for drinks and snacks all at once, and one harassed mother trying to get them to order one at a time, so I have to get to work. Valentín really gets the hang of pouring drinks after a few minor incidents, but I still feel that it's a little crowded back here. I'm hoping that he'll get tired of the work and quit — it seems to take a lot of mental effort for him to do more than one simple thing at a time. After we fill the orders, he sits down on a box in the far corner and closes his eyes. It must be tough to have to work so hard at every little thing you do. He catches me staring at him while he takes the rubber-band ball he's been working on out of his pocket and starts a tail or a leg on it. But he just smiles at me and a peaceful look settles over his face. I guess that means he's happy.

Everything settles into a routine for Valentín and me for the next few days. The only problem I have is Mrs. O'Brien, who calls me a lot to ask me about him and about Bob Dylan. I just say everything's okay, even though Bob Dylan has zeroed in on an older girl, actually, somebody I know from El Building, and he's disappeared with her at least once that I know of. I found out after she left her two-year-old son alone, asleep on a lounge chair. When he woke up, he started crying so loud that I had to go out there and get him before someone called Mrs. O'Brien. I brought him into the store, and it was instant friendship between the kid and Valentín. Valentín sat down on the floor with Pablito, who told us his name after he calmed down. The two of them played with the rubber-band animals until his mother, Maricela Nuñez, finally showed up looking like she'd been having a good time. Her hair was a mess, and she had grass stains on her white T-shirt and shorts. I was furious.

"Is Pablito having fun with his new friend?" she says in a fake-friendly voice, showing no anxiety over the fact that the kid could have drowned or just walked off into traffic while she was in the woods fooling around with Bob Dylan. But Maricela is a special case. She practically brought herself up when her mother left her and her father years ago, and her old man was never home either. She dropped out of school in tenth grade and had Pablito a few months later. Now she works at night at the Caribbean Moon nightclub as a cocktail waitress, while her father stays with the kid; and she spends her afternoons on the front stoop of our building flirting with the men who hang out there. She's staking out the pool now, where she's working on Bob Dylan. I heard that she called him her "boy toy" the other day from someone I know in my building, Anita, who is also fast-tracking her life, taking lessons from the champ, Maricela.

My mother uses Maricela as a warning to me of what I'll become if I don't get an education and stay away from boys. I sometimes remind my mother that if Maricela's parents had given her a good home life, maybe she would have turned out better. But now, seeing her standing there looking totally unconcerned about the danger her son could have faced in the last hour, makes me want to turn her in to family services. She doesn't deserve to have a cute little kid like Pablito.

"Look at them," she says, laughing at the way Pablito and Valentín are lining up the animals back on the counter. "I think Pablito is teaching the dummy a few things."

Valentín looks at me with such a hurt expression on his face that I honestly had to count to five or I would have punched her. Pablito tries to get Valentín's attention by pulling on his pants leg, but Valentín just says, "*Trabajo*," and goes back to his newest project. Pablito starts crying and yelling, "Tin, Tin," which is the part of Valentín's name he had picked up. I lift him over the counter to his mother. "Maricela, I really think that you are the dummy. You listen up. If we hadn't been here to take care of your son, someone would have called the family services and they would have taken him away — which may be the best thing for him anyway." I'd heard my mother say that was just what'll end up happening to poor Pablito.

"You're just jealous, *niña*. You can't stand the competition. And, little girl, nobody is going to take Pablito away from me. Have you noticed that he looks a little like Bob Dylan?" she says, laughing.

I lean over the counter so that my face is right in front of her face. "Why do you ask, Maricela? Are you having trouble remembering who the father is?" I hiss at her.

She storms off, and behind me I hear soft laughter. It's Valentín, apparently amusing himself with his new toy.

By Friday afternoon, Clarissa, Anne, and I have gotten the message from Bob Dylan's attitude that he is not interested in our company. Maricela has been here every afternoon, and she, Pablito, and Bob Dylan leave together. I see my summer turning into a boring routine, since Anne and Clarissa are mad at Bob Dylan and are staying away from the pool. Valentín is getting good at pouring drinks and cleaning up, so at least the job is easier. The rest of the time he works with his rubber bands and only talks when Maricela brings Pablito over for a snack.

Valentín is teaching Pablito the names of his animals in Spanish. Maricela has nothing to say to me, but she does hang around for a while when Valentín and her son become absorbed in their daily game. "*Elefante, caballo, oso*"— Valentín points to each animal; then Pablito tries to repeat the words. This makes

Valentín smile big. I guess it makes him feel good to be able to teach someone else something for a change.

It's almost closing time on Friday and I'm counting bags of potato chips, candy bars, and other snack stuff while Valentín is checking to see how much soda mix is left in the back, when we hear a kind of little scream. It doesn't last long, so I almost ignore it, thinking it's some kid out in the street, since the pool is supposed to be closed for the day. But Valentín has come out with a really scared look on his face and is leaning way out over the counter trying to see something in the water. I don't see anything, but Valentín is flapping his arms like he's trying to take off and stuttering "Pa . . . Pa . . . Pa . . ." I can't understand him. His tongue seems to be getting twisted around the words he's trying to say, and his eyes look terrified. I start thinking he may be about to have a fit or something.

"What is it, Valentín?" I put my hand on his arm like Mrs. O'Brien does when she walks him home in the afternoon. I figure it calms him down. "What do you see out there?"

"Pablito. Pablito." He is trembling so much I fear he's going to go out of control. But I don't have time to think, the water *is* moving, and it could be the kid. I don't see Bob Dylan anywhere.

"Get Mrs. O'Brien!" I yell to Valentín as I run out. But he is frozen on the spot.

When I get to the pool, I see the kid is thrashing wildly near the edge. He's really scared, and his kicking is only forcing him away toward the deep water. I jump into the shallow end and start walking in his direction. I cannot tell how deep it will be as I take each step, and I feel scared that it will be over my head before I know it. My mother's words of warning come back to me. I may drown, but I have to reach Pablito. I keep going toward his voice. But I feel that I'm moving in slow motion, so I finally dive into the water. My glasses get wet and I can't see, so I throw them off, which makes it worse. I can't see a thing. I start screaming for help, hoping that Bob Dylan or Mrs. O'Brien will hear me. My lungs are about to explode and I'm sinking and pushing up, stretching my hands in front of me in case I feel his body. Suddenly I find myself at the edge of the deep end of the pool and I hold on, trying to catch my breath.

I am screaming hysterically by then. But just when I feel that my lungs are going to burst, I feel Pablito's little legs wrapping themselves around my waist. I pull him up, and he grabs a handful of my hair. He is like a baby monkey holding on to his mama. I hear splashing behind me, and it's Valentín heading for us. He carries Pablito out of the pool in one arm and pulls me out with his free hand.

When I take him from Valentín's arms, his body feels limp, so I put him on the ground and push on his tiny chest until water comes out. Soon he is coughing and crying.

While I am frantically doing what I can for him, Valentín holds Pablito's hand and talks to him in Spanish. Then I see Bob Dylan and Maricela run up. Bob Dylan takes over the chest compressions while I run to call Mrs. O'Brien and the emergency rescue. Maricela goes nuts. She keeps calling out for her baby and trying to get to him, until Valentín guides her to a bench, where they sit holding hands until the ambulance drives up. She and Bob Dylan ride with Pablito to the hospital.

It's all over in minutes, but I feel like it's days while Valentín and I sit in Mrs. O'Brien's office wrapped in big towels, waiting for word from the hospital. I also expect to get fired for not reporting that Bob Dylan was not at his post like Mrs. O'Brien had warned me to do.

She comes in in a very solemn mood, and I look over at Valentín, who is wringing his hands. I know he's only thinking of Pablito, and I feel a little guilty for worrying about myself so much.

"The boy is going to be fine," Mrs. O'Brien says, "thanks to both of you."

Then she does something that really surprises me. She comes over and kisses me on the forehead. I am cold and shivering, and I sneeze practically in her face. "Sorry," I say, feeling a little bit stupid. She fishes my foggy glasses out of her skirt pocket. I busy myself cleaning the lenses on my wet towel.

"We have to get you into some dry clothes," she says. Then she goes over to Valentín, who is fidgeting with a rubber-band animal that has become a sort of wet brown lump.

"Valentín, you did a very good thing today. You and Teresa saved a little boy's life. You are a hero. Do you understand me?"

"*Sí,*" Valentín says. But I'm not sure about his English, so I start to translate: "Valentín, *ella dice que eres un héroe.*"

"I know," Valentín says, and smiles real big.

"You speak English?" I cannot believe he's fooled me into thinking that he can barely speak a few words of Spanish, and here he understands two languages.

"*Sí,*" Valentín answers, and laughs his funny quiet laugh.

Mrs. O'Brien looks at Valentín in a motherly way. "Valentín, how would you like to keep your job here year-round?"

Valentín has been just staring at his hands as she talks, almost like he was not listening. But then he slowly glances over at me, as if asking me what I think. He can communicate in total silence, and I'm learning his language.

"When the pool closes at the end of the summer, we are going to ask you, and yes, Teresa too, to come work in my office. We have many things that you both can do, such as helping out with after-school programs and supervising the playground. Are you interested?"

Valentín looks at me for an answer again. I can tell that we have to take the job as partners or he won't do it. I sneeze loudly, and he practically falls out of his chair. Really, he's the most nervous human being I've ever met. I see that I'm going to have to put up with him in this new job too. I don't think anyone else would have the patience.

# Glossary of Spanish Terms
## in "A Job for Valentín"

El Building: The Building

*Soy Valentín:* I am Valentín

*sí:* yes

*trabajo:* work

*animales:* animals

*el hombre:* the man

*siempre:* always

*dos dólares:* two dollars

*gracias:* thank you

*niña:* girl

*elefante, caballo, oso:* elephant, horse, bear

*Ella dice que eres un héroe:* She says that you are a hero

# The No-Guitar Blues

Gary Soto

The moment Fausto saw the group Los Lobos on *American Bandstand,* he knew exactly what he wanted to do with his life — play guitar. His eyes grew large with excitement as Los Lobos ground out a song while teenagers bounced off each other on the crowded dance floor.

He had watched *American Bandstand* for years and had heard Ray Camacho and the Teardrops at Romain Playground, but it had never occurred to him that he too might become a musician. That afternoon Fausto knew his mission in life: to play guitar in his own band; to sweat out his songs and prance around the stage; to make money and dress weird.

Fausto turned off the television set and walked outside, wondering how he could get enough money to buy a guitar. He couldn't ask his parents because they would just say, "Money doesn't grow on trees" or "What do you think we are, bankers?" And besides, they hated rock music. They were into the *conjunto* music of Lydia Mendoza, Flaco Jimenez, and Little Joe and La Familia. And, as Fausto recalled, the last album they bought was *The Chipmunks Sing Christmas Favorites.*

But what the heck, he'd give it a try. He returned inside and watched his mother make tortillas. He leaned against the kitchen counter, trying to work up the nerve to ask her for a guitar. Finally, he couldn't hold back any longer.

"Mom," he said, "I want a guitar for Christmas."

She looked up from rolling tortillas. "Honey, a guitar costs a lot of money."

"How 'bout for my birthday next year," he tried again.

"I can't promise," she said, turning back to her tortillas, "but we'll see."

Fausto walked back outside with a buttered tortilla. He knew his mother was right. His father was a warehouseman at Berven Rugs, where he made good money but not enough to buy everything his children wanted. Fausto decided to mow lawns to earn money, and was pushing the mower down the street before he realized it was winter and no one would hire him. He returned the mower and picked up a rake. He hopped onto his sister's bike (his had two flat tires) and rode north to the nicer section of Fresno in search of work. He went door-to-door, but after three hours he managed to get only one job, and not to rake leaves. He was asked to hurry down to the store to buy a loaf of bread, for which he received a grimy, dirt-caked quarter.

He also got an orange, which he ate sitting at the curb. While he was eating, a dog walked up and sniffed his leg. Fausto pushed him away and threw an orange peel skyward. The dog caught it and ate it in one gulp. The dog looked at Fausto and wagged his tail for more. Fausto tossed him a slice of orange, and the dog snapped it up and licked his lips.

"How come you like oranges, dog?"

The dog blinked a pair of sad eyes and whined.

"What's the matter? Cat got your tongue?" Fausto laughed at his joke and offered the dog another slice.

At that moment a dim light came on inside Fausto's head. He saw that it was sort of a fancy dog, a terrier or something, with dog tags and a shiny collar. And it looked well fed and healthy. In his neighborhood, the dogs were never licensed, and if they got sick they were placed near the water heater until they got well.

This dog looked like he belonged to rich people. Fausto cleaned his juice-sticky hands on his pants and got to his feet. The light in his head grew brighter. It just might work. He called the dog, patted its muscular back, and bent down to check the license.

"Great," he said. "There's an address."

The dog's name was Roger, which struck Fausto as weird because he'd never heard of a dog with a human name. Dogs should have names like Bomber, Freckles, Queenie, Killer, and Zero.

Fausto planned to take the dog home and collect a reward. He would say he had found Roger near the freeway. That would scare the daylights out of the owners, who would be so happy that they would probably give him a reward. He felt bad about lying, but the dog *was* loose. And it might even really be lost, because the address was six blocks away.

Fausto stashed the rake and his sister's bike behind a bush, and, tossing an orange peel every time Roger became distracted, walked the dog to his house. He hesitated on the porch until Roger began to scratch the door with a muddy paw. Fausto had come this far, so he figured he might as well go through with it. He knocked softly. When no one answered, he rang the doorbell. A man in a silky bathrobe and slippers opened the door and seemed confused by the sight of his dog and the boy.

"Sir," Fausto said, gripping Roger by the collar. "I found your dog by the freeway. His dog license says he lives here."

Gary Soto

Fausto looked down at the dog, then up to the man. "He does, doesn't he?"

The man stared at Fausto a long time before saying in a pleasant voice, "That's right." He pulled his robe tighter around him because of the cold and asked Fausto to come in. "So he was by the freeway?"

"Uh-huh."

"You bad, snoopy dog," said the man, wagging his finger. "You probably knocked over some trash cans, too, didn't you?"

Fausto didn't say anything. He looked around, amazed by this house with its shiny furniture and a television as large as the front window at home. Warm bread smells filled the air, and music full of soft tinkling floated in from another room.

"Helen," the man called to the kitchen. "We have a visitor." His wife came into the living room, wiping her hands on a dish towel and smiling. "And who have we here?" she asked in one of the softest voices Fausto had ever heard.

"This young man said he found Roger near the freeway."

Fausto repeated his story to her while staring at a perpetual clock with a bell-shaped glass, the kind his aunt got when she celebrated her twenty-fifth anniversary. The lady frowned and said, wagging a finger at Roger, "Oh, you're a bad boy."

"It was very nice of you to bring Roger home," the man said. "Where do you live?"

"By that vacant lot on Olive," he said. "You know, by Brownie's Flower Place."

The wife looked at her husband, then Fausto. Her eyes twinkled triangles of light as she said, "Well, young man, you're probably hungry. How about a turnover?"

"What do I have to turn over?" Fausto asked, thinking she was talking about yard work or something like turning trays of dried raisins.

"No, no, dear, it's a pastry." She took him by the elbow and guided him to a kitchen that sparkled with copper pans and bright yellow wallpaper. She guided him to the kitchen table and gave him a tall glass of milk and something that looked like an *empanada*. Steamy waves of heat escaped when he tore it in two. He ate with both eyes on the man and woman who stood arm-in-arm smiling at him. They were strange, he thought. But nice.

"That was good," he said after he finished the turnover. "Did you make it, ma'am?"

"Yes, I did. Would you like another?"

"No, thank you. I have to go home now."

As Fausto walked to the door, the man opened his wallet and took out a bill. "This is for you," he said. "Roger is special to us, almost like a son."

Fausto looked at the bill and knew he was in trouble. Not with these nice folks or with his parents but with himself. How could he have been so deceitful? The dog wasn't lost. It was just having a fun Saturday walking around.

"I can't take that."

"You have to. You deserve it, believe me," the man said.

"No, I don't."

"Now, don't be silly," said the lady. She took the bill from her husband and stuffed it into Fausto's shirt pocket. "You're a lovely child. Your parents are lucky to have you. Be good. And come see us again, please."

Fausto went out, and the lady closed the door. Fausto clutched the bill through his shirt pocket. He felt like ringing the doorbell and begging them to please take the money back, but he knew they would refuse. He hurried away and, at the end of the block, pulled the bill from his shirt pocket: It was a crisp twenty-dollar bill.

"Oh, man, I shouldn't have lied," he said under his breath

as he started up the street like a zombie. He wanted to run to church for Saturday confession, but it was past four-thirty, when confession stopped.

He returned to the bush where he had hidden the rake and his sister's bike and rode home slowly, not daring to touch the money in his pocket. At home, in the privacy of his room, he examined the twenty-dollar bill. He had never had so much money. It was probably enough to buy a secondhand guitar. But he felt bad, like the time he stole a dollar from the secret fold inside his older brother's wallet.

Fausto went outside and sat on the fence. "Yeah," he said. "I can probably get a guitar for twenty. Maybe at a yard sale — things are cheaper."

His mother called him to dinner.

The next day he dressed for church without anyone telling him. He was going to go to eight o'clock mass.

"I'm going to church, Mom," he said. His mother was in the kitchen cooking *papas* and *chorizo con huevos.* A pile of tortillas lay warm under a dish towel.

"Oh, I'm so proud of you, son." She beamed, turning over the crackling *papas.*

His older brother, Lawrence, who was at the table reading the funnies, mimicked, "Oh, I'm so proud of you, son," under his breath.

At Saint Theresa's he sat near the front. When Father Jerry began by saying that we are all sinners, Fausto thought he looked right at him. Could he know? Fausto fidgeted with guilt. No, he thought. I only did it yesterday.

Fausto knelt, prayed, and sang. But he couldn't forget the man and the lady, whose names he didn't even know, and the *empanada* they had given him. It had a strange name but tasted really good. He wondered how they got rich. And how that dome clock worked. He had asked his mother once how his aunt's clock worked. She said it just worked, the way the refrigerator works. It just did.

Fausto caught his mind wandering and tried to concentrate on his sins. He said a Hail Mary and sang, and when the wicker basket came his way, he stuck a hand reluctantly in his pocket and pulled out the twenty-dollar bill. He ironed it between his palms, and dropped it into the basket. The grown-ups stared. Here was a kid dropping twenty dollars in the basket while they gave just three or four dollars.

There would be a second collection for Saint Vincent de Paul, the lector announced. The wicker baskets again floated in the pews, and this time the adults around him, given a second chance to show their charity, dug deep into their wallets and purses and dropped in fives and tens. This time Fausto tossed in the grimy quarter.

Fausto felt better after church. He went home and played football in the front yard with his brother and some neighbor kids. He felt cleared of wrongdoing and was so happy that he played one of his best games of football ever. On one play, he tore his good pants, which he knew he shouldn't have been wearing. For a second, while he examined the hole, he wished he hadn't given the twenty dollars away.

Man, I coulda bought me some Levis, he thought. He pictured his twenty dollars being spent to buy church candles. He pictured a priest buying an armful of flowers with *his* money.

Fausto had to forget about getting a guitar. He spent the next day playing soccer in his good pants, which were now his old pants. But that night during dinner, his mother said she remembered seeing an old bass *guitarron* the last time she cleaned out her father's garage.

"It's a little dusty," his mom said, serving his favorite enchiladas, "but I think it works. Grandpa says it works."

Fausto's ears perked up. That was the same kind the guy in

Gary Soto

Los Lobos played. Instead of asking for the guitar, he waited for his mother to offer it to him. And she did, while gathering the dishes from the table.

"No, Mom, I'll do it," he said, hugging her. "I'll do the dishes forever if you want."

It was the happiest day of his life. No, it was the second-happiest day of his life. The happiest was when his grandfather Lupe placed the *guitarron,* which was nearly as huge as a wash-tub, in his arms. Fausto ran a thumb down the strings, which vibrated in his throat and chest. It sounded beautiful, deep and eerie. A pumpkin smile widened on his face.

"OK, *hijo,* now you put your fingers like this," said his grand-father, smelling of tobacco and aftershave. He took Fausto's fingers and placed them on the strings. Fausto strummed a chord on the *guitarron,* and the bass resounded in their chests.

The *guitarron* was more complicated than Fausto had imag-ined. But he was confident that after a few more lessons he could start a band that would someday play on *American Bandstand* for the dancing crowds.

# Hands in the Darkness

Peter D. Sieruta

I always thought I could talk my way out of *anything*. But when a cop is sticking his face through the car window and blinding your eyes with a high-beam flashlight, words don't come quick. Especially when the car you're riding in isn't yours. Especially when you've got a bottle of something illegal in your hand.

By the time we got to the police station, I had a great story worked out. I said I didn't know the car was stolen when Stewie drove up in it. That the bottle was really his; I was just holding it for him. But then they gave me a blood test — and you can't talk your way out of that. They call it "state's evidence."

A few weeks later, when we went to court, the judge tried to scare us. He talked about how a lot of us "youthful offenders" don't even make it to our eighteenth birthdays. I counted out the months by pressing my fingers into the sides of my jeans. I would be eighteen in twenty-seven months. If I only had twenty-seven months to live, I wanted to do it *outside* jail, so I tried to look really innocent.

It only took ten minutes before they sentenced Stewie to a youth home. Because he had a record for borrowing cars that didn't belong to him. And it probably didn't help that he kept calling the judge "dude."

My innocent look must've worked, because I didn't get sent away. Instead, I got community service.

I also got a social worker.

When we met, Mrs. Gibb introduced herself and held out her hand. I pretended I didn't notice and walked around it. But I didn't want her to think I was unfriendly, so I started talking about what a good view of the interstate she had from her office window.

She said, "Well, Gaston —" and I broke in right away: "Don't ever call me that name." *That name.* I won't even say it out loud. My mom got it from a thick paperback book called *Love's Blazing Embers,* and I'll never forgive her. If I do live to be eighteen, I'm going to change it first thing.

Mrs. Gibb said, "What should I call you?"

I said, "I like it when people use my last name." My last name is Major, and *that* is a very cool name.

"Well, Major, I think we should be very grateful to Judge Tomlinson."

"For what?"

"For giving you this second chance."

"I was innocent!" I shouted.

She picked up a file with my name on it. We both knew those blood test results were in there. She looked at me for a second, then said, "I'm sure he considered the fact that you've had no previous arrests and that you've done fairly well in school . . . despite attendance problems."

I said, "When I'm at school, I'm great."

She said, "What about when you're not at school?"

"I'm still great," I said. "But in a different way."

"Mandatory attendance is one of the terms of your sentence. I'll be calling your school every Friday for an attendance report."

I knew this much about adults: She'd never do it. Well, maybe she'd call the first Friday. But she'd forget for a couple weeks before she called the second time. After that she'd never call again. I figured this community service was the same way. I'd do whatever they told me — fill potholes in the street, wash the courthouse windows — for a few weeks until they forgot about me and I could quit going.

It wasn't such a bad deal.

But when Gibby started talking about my community service, she didn't say anything about potholes or window washing. Instead, it was all people stuff. Helping out in a day care center. Visiting hospital patients. Working with retards. I said, "I hate people stuff."

"Well, Gast —"

I glared.

"Well, Major, just about everything in the world involves people." She picked up a card from her desk and said, "Would you enjoy working with the elderly?"

"Am I supposed to *enjoy* this?"

"We could arrange your community service at the Middlegate Retirement Plaza."

"That might be cool," I said, because it sounded like a very classy place. I pictured a big hotel with a fountain in the lobby and old people dressed up fancy, drinking tea and chowing down on sugar cookies. They'd probably have me pouring tea and toting trays. I could live with that.

Mrs. Gibb said, "You've been given two hundred hours of community service. How should we divide that up?"

"How about one hour a year for two hundred years?"

"Let's make that four hours a week for *one* year," she said. "Maybe right after school?"

But I told her I'd rather do my community service at nighttime. My mom and stepfather (number three) liked to drink at night, and I tried to stay out of their way. And I decided to do it Monday through Thursday, because on the weekends I can usually find *someone* to hang out with. Even if I hardly know them.

Mrs. Gibb gave me an orange card for the people at the Middlegate Retirement Plaza to sign each time I went in. When we were all finished, she stood up and said, "Good luck, Major. I'll see you in two weeks." I thought she might try to shake my hand again, so I said, "Thanks" as fast as I could and shot out the door.

On Monday night, I walked to the Middlegate Retirement Plaza, kicking up piles of dead leaves. But as I got closer and closer, there were less and less leaves. That's because the Middlegate Retirement Plaza was almost downtown, on a street without trees or grass. It was a long, low building sitting tight between Burger King and Hampton's Auto Parts — New and Used.

The light in front of the building was burned out, but from what I could see, the outside didn't look very fancy . . . and the inside was even worse. For one thing, it smelled. It smelled *terrible*. And there weren't any windows in the lobby, just walls painted the color of green mouthwash. In the center of the room was a big desk with a big nurse behind it.

This nurse was smiling. Her bright yellow hair was pulled back tight, taking her face with it — so her shiny red lips stretched almost all the way to her ears. She watched me walk across the lobby without saying a word.

I said, "Hey, how you doing?"

She said, "May I help you, ma'am?"

"I. Am. Not. A. Girl."

"Really?" she said, like it was a big surprise.

I said, "No, lady, I'm not!"

"Well!" she said. "With that long hair and all those earrings . . ."

"What do I gotta do, lady, drop my drawers?"

"Well!" she said. "I am going to write that down!" It was funny how only her bottom lip moved when she talked. And how she kept smiling the whole time. She got a pad and wrote something. I read it upside down: *What do I have to do? lady? Drop my draws.*

I was only in tenth grade, but even I knew how to spell *drawers.*

I said, "Why'd you write that down?"

"We will just see how Mrs. Gibb feels about your smart mouth when she reads this," she said.

Since I never told her who I was, I couldn't figure how she knew about Gibby or why I was there. But then I decided it was pretty obvious who I was, since not too many people under a hundred years old came into that place voluntarily.

I said, "You're supposed to sign this," and handed her the orange card.

She said, "Would you please sign this card, Ms. Otis?"

"Would you please sign this card, Ms. Otis?" I repeated, feeling my toenails scrape the insides of my Nikes.

"That's better," she said, then signed her name: *B. Otis, Nurse's Aide.*

I should've guessed this woman was no nurse. Nurses are nice. Her very next question was "Do you know how to read?"

"Do *you?*" I said, and while she was writing *that* down, I told her, "I can read great."

"The last delinquent we had working here couldn't read at all, so I had him empty bedpans."

Even the judge didn't call me a delinquent.

The nurse's aide got up, and I followed her down the hall. She walked very straight, but her head swung from side to side as she passed each open door. In the first room, about five old people were crowded around a black-and-white TV watching *Jeopardy!* The rest of the rooms had old people sitting on the sides of their beds in sweaters and pants or lying down in their pj's. One lady with fluffy white hair like a cloud pinned to her head was sleeping in a wheelchair in the hallway. B. Otis swooped down on her like a smiling vulture. "Mrs. Wysocki! You are BLOCKING the hallway. You are CREATING a fire hazard!" She pointed me toward the last door on the left and said, "Go read the newspaper to Mr. Diggs. I'll check on you later." She took off, pushing the sleeping lady down the hall, and I knew she'd forget to ever come back.

The room at the end of the hall had two names masking-taped to the door: Mr. William Diggs and Mr. Bert Czarnowiak. At least my guy had the easy name. Inside, the room was dark, with only a small lamp between the two beds. One man was putting on a robe and whistling. The other was lying there like a corpse. I said, "One of you dudes named Willie Diggs?"

The man with the robe said, "Hee-hee-hee, this boy is asking for *you,* Mr. Diggs."

So Diggs was the corpse.

I got closer and saw he was a small, shriveled black man. I was glad, because if you've ever seen any movies, you know that old black men are *very* cool, and always tell kids all kinds of wise and worthwhile junk.

"Hey, how you doing?" I said to him, but he didn't answer.

"Talk louder," said Bert Czarnowiak. "He's blind."

"HEY, HOW YOU DOING?" I yelled.

"I'm blind, not deaf," said Mr. Diggs, in a quiet but mean voice.

76

I glared at Czarnowiak, then said to Diggs, "You didn't answer when I said it the first time."

"He never answers no one," said Czarnowiak.

"Then why'd you tell me to talk louder?"

Bert Czarnowiak shrugged. He was beginning to tick me off.

"My name's Major," I said.

"I don't think we should call you that," said Czarnowiak.

I got a sick feeling that Gibb had phoned ahead and told everyone to call me Gaston. I said, "Why's that?"

"You look more like a *minor*, hee-hee-hee."

I turned my back on him and said to Mr. Diggs, "That lady at the desk — B. Otis — said I gotta read you a newspaper."

"Then shut up and read it," said Diggs.

He dug around his covers, trying to grab ahold of the paper. I could see it lying by his knee, all wrapped up tight in brown paper, but I wasn't about to tell him where it was. Not after he told me to shut up.

I went to the window and peeked behind the rickety shade. The parking lot at Burger King was lighted up so I could see the trash compactor right outside the window. A girl in a BK uniform was dumping plastic bags of garbage and smoking a cigarette. "You guys ever sneak out here for a Whopper?" I asked.

"The windows are nailed shut," said Mr. Czarnowiak.

I felt around the windowsill, through all kinds of dust and dirt and crunchy dead insects, until my fingers scraped against the nails. "What happens if you need to get out?" I said. "If there's a fire or something?"

"Then we die," said Czarnowiak. "Hee-hee-hee."

I felt like asking him what was so funny about dying in a fire. But just then he said, "I'm going to play *Jeopardy!*" and hurried out of the room.

"What a moron," I said to Mr. Diggs.

He didn't answer. He just held out the newspaper in my direction.

I grabbed the paper, then dragged over a folded metal chair that was leaning against a wall. But when I tried to open it up, it turned out to be one of those walkers that old people use. "Aren't there any chairs around here?" I asked.

"You're the one with eyes," he said. "Go look for one."

That old man had an *attitude!*

Before I went looking for a chair, I tested to see how blind he really was. I stuck out my tongue. Pretended to throw the newspaper at him. Made some gestures I knew he wouldn't appreciate. Nothing seemed to make a difference.

There weren't any extra chairs lying around — the room was too small for that — but I finally found one in about the strangest place you could think of. Next to Czarnowiak's bed was a door leading to a tiny bathroom, and there in the middle of the *tub* was this metal bench. I carried it into the room and set it beside Mr. Diggs's bed.

I peeled the brown paper from the *Detroit Free Press* and said, "Detroit? Is that where you're from?" He didn't answer. I said, "I never been there. I never even been out of Ohio." He still didn't answer, so I tried one last time: "You're probably wondering why a kid like me is working here, right?"

"No," he said.

I glared, but that doesn't really work if the other person can't see. So I rattled the newspaper as much as I could when I opened it up and spread it on the side of his bed. The headline said, "District Court Issues Ruling on Bond Plan." Underneath that was another story, "Utility Commission Findings Made Public," and beside that was "Unemployment Rates Rise for Second Month."

"Exciting place," I said, then started reading out loud about that bond issue. Diggs raised his hand in the air to stop me. "You start with the obituaries," he said. He didn't say, "Please start with the obituaries" or "Will you start with the obituaries?"

I made that growling sound in my throat that all my teachers hate and turned to page D-18. At first it was interesting to see all the ways people could die, but after reading about Ruth Addams, Emmett Barkley, James Carr, and Samuel E. Chandler, I was beginning to get sick of this death stuff. "Ernestine Deacon," I read. "Dear wife of the late Stephen. Loving mother of Stephen Jr., Caroline, Ellen, and —"

Just then I heard this rattling sound. It was coming from under the old man's bed. "What's that?" I said.

"Keep reading," he said.

"What's that noise?" It sounded like crumpled paper rolling across the wooden floor.

"Rat or a mouse," he said, like it was no big deal.

"No way!" I said, but pulled my feet off the floor and crossed them in my lap just in case. I don't mind mice, but rats . . . ! I leaned forward to look into his face, to see if he was putting me on, but he wasn't smiling or laughing. He was just staring straight up at the ceiling with his dead eyes. What was *with* this old guy? I leaned even closer and fell right off the stool, landing on my knees and hands. As I knelt there with my hands pressed into the sticky floor, I felt something run past my fingers. I yelled and jumped. There was a snort from the bed, but when I looked at Diggs, the expression on his face hadn't changed at all.

I bent down and wiggled my fingers on his pillow. I said, "Hey, Willie Diggs, there's a big old rat crawling by your face."

I thought he'd freak or scream or pee his pj's.

Instead, his hand flew across that bed and slammed down on top of mine. He didn't say a word, just pressed so hard I could feel past the pillow, past the sheets, all the way down to the springs in the mattress. "Leggo, leggo!" I shouted, my voice getting desperate. He wasn't hurting me. *Nothing* hurts me. But I learned a long time ago that nobody's got a right to touch you without your permission, and that's just what he was doing.

"Let go! Let go of me!" I almost said "please," and I never *ever* say that. But I couldn't pull away; that old dude was *strong*. I don't know how long he held on to my hand, but as soon as he let go, I took off running.

In the visitors' john, I scrubbed my hands forever. They had the kind of soap that burns when you use it, and I was glad. The paper toweling broke into a million pieces when I tried to dry my hands, so I just used the front of my T-shirt.

Back in the lobby, B. Otis was reading *Time* magazine and smoking a Virginia Slim. She looked up like she never saw me before.

I said, "I don't mind reading to these old people, but tell them to keep their hands to themselves!"

"What are you talking about?"

"That old man grabbed me and wouldn't let go."

"That's nonsense," she said. "And I'm writing it down for Mrs. Gibb."

B. Otis wrote down everything I ever said to her. And then she mailed her notes to Mrs. Gibb. At the end of the week, Gibby called me to find out why I was screwing up. "What's this I hear about you calling Ms. Otis a drug pusher?" she asked. I had to think for a second to remember what I really said; B. Otis always twisted my words around. "I didn't say she was a drug pusher," I told Mrs. Gibb. "I said she gives the patients too many drugs. There's a difference."

But it wasn't a big difference. The patients at Middlegate Retirement Plaza took more dope in one day than I had in

my entire life. When I went to work on Tuesday, I was glad I
didn't have to read to Mr. Diggs. Instead I was assigned to Mrs.
Wysocki, that old lady who was sleeping in the hallway the first
night. I said, "My name's Major," and she said, "How nice!"

I said, "I'm supposed to read to you," and she said, "How
nice!"

I picked up *Ladies Home Journal,* and she said, "How
nice!"

Then she fell asleep before I even started reading and *I* said,
"How nice!" I snuck out for some fries at Burger King, and
B. Otis bawled me out when I came back. I think that's when
I told her the patients slept so much because she gave them
too many drugs.

The next night, I was assigned to some old man whose name
I can't remember. He wanted me to read him the Bible. When
I told him it had too many hard words and that I didn't understand what any of it meant, he wanted me to say a prayer with
him and then started swearing at me when I wouldn't. Later,
he told B. Otis he never wanted to see "that heathen" (me)
ever again.

So on Thursday, Otis sent me to this old lady, who handed
me a beat-up paperback book that was like a thousand pages
long. I glared, then started reading the first chapter, which had
more *thee*s *and thou*s in it than the Bible. Then I got to the word
*Gaston* and choked. I looked at the front cover and saw the title
was *Love's Blazing Embers.*

"And then you threw the book at her," said Mrs. Gibb on
the telephone.

"I did not! I didn't hit her. I didn't even try to hit her! I
threw it at the *other* wall!"

Gibby sighed. "Well, Ms. Otis is quite unhappy with your
work so far. She said there's only one patient who's willing to
give you another chance. I understand he's a bit hard to get

along with, but he seldom gets visitors, and he very much wants someone to read to him."

I should have known from the description that I was stuck with Mr. Diggs again.

So on Monday night, I returned to his room and said, "I'm back."

"Start reading," he said, sounding meaner than ever.

From then on, Willie Diggs was my permanent assignment. He was my punishment for riding around drunk in that stolen car, for skipping out to Burger King, for refusing to pray, and for throwing books. Night after night I had to read the *Detroit Free Press* to an old man who never talked, never smiled, and didn't give a damn about me at all. I spent a lot of time counting how many months were left in my sentence.

Mrs. Gibb said, "Major, this job is a wonderful opportunity. If you just give Mr. Diggs a chance, I'm sure you'll find out you have a lot in common. Talk to him. Listen to him."

I talked my head off, but it didn't do any good. And I listened . . . but the only things he ever said to me were "Yes," "No," "Shut up," "Read the paper," and "I don't care."

I don't think he cared about *anything*. Well, maybe he cared about the *Detroit Free Press*. Why else did he special order it all the way from Detroit when he couldn't even afford a new pair of pajamas? He must have cared about the obits and bond issues and court cases, even though his expression never changed as I read each article. But why?

Even though I didn't like Willie Diggs, I didn't want to think his whole life had been awful. So I made up some cool stories about him in my head. Like he used to be a famous baseball player. Or he was married to a beautiful lady and had a bunch of kids. But then I'd think, If he's famous, what's he doing at this place? If he's got a family, why don't they ever come see him? Sometimes when I was reading him an article, I'd stop in the middle of a sentence and just stare at his face. Nobody could be that quiet. I kept thinking that one day he'd just explode.

But I was the one who ended up exploding.

It was the last really warm night that fall. Of course the Middlegate Retirement Plaza didn't have air-conditioning. The pages of the newspaper were sticking together, and I almost couldn't breathe from the smell of rubbing alcohol and dirty bathrooms and something else I couldn't exactly figure out but always thought must be what death smelled like. The rattling under the bed was louder than ever. Diggs didn't seem to notice.

I was reading him an article called "Teens in Trouble," about some Detroit kids who went to a special "at-risk high school" because they'd been in trouble with the law. Sounded better than working in a retirement home.

The rattling under the bed was starting to rattle me. I even made a mistake when I was reading, and I *never* do that. I tried to take a deep breath but choked on the smell. I said, "Hey, Mr. Diggs, you ever know a teen who was in trouble?" When he didn't answer, I got even louder. "Well, I guess you know *me*, right? You want to hear about trouble? My mom got married four times and drinks a lot and, worst of all, she named me Gaston. You wouldn't believe how some of her husbands treated me! I got arrested in a stolen car when I was drunk and I don't have any friends and every single thing I say out loud gets copied down by B. Otis and I hear about it again from Mrs. Gibb, who's my social worker."

When he still didn't say anything, I pounded my fist down as hard as I could on the metal stool and ran from the room.

In the lobby, B. Otis was dozing off in front of a *Family Circle* magazine. Yes, she even smiled in her sleep. I stopped at her desk and slammed my hands down. "What's wrong with him?" I shouted.

She jerked awake. "What? *Who?*"

"Willie Diggs. What's his story? Where does he come from? Why is he here? Who is he?"

"EXCUSE me?" she said, like it was none of my business. "We do have client confidentiality rules, you know!"

I said, "I been coming in here for over a month, and I don't know one thing about him. Does he have kids? Was he married? What work did he do? Why is he so mad all the time?"

She smiled and said, "He's just a tired old man, waiting to die."

I felt like writing that down and sending it to *her* boss.

The next night was Halloween, and I had to stomp through puddles and bend my head against the wind as I walked to the Middlegate Retirement Plaza. But the rain and cold didn't stop the trick-or-treaters, who wore coats over their costumes and carried wet pillowcases for their treats. A lot of kids were stopping at Burger King, 'cause they were handing out free gift certificates. One little kid only about eight years old came out of the BK, wearing a clown mask and dragging his pillowcase behind him. He was walking across the parking lot all by himself when an older kid jumped from behind a parked car, grabbed the boy's bag, and came running down the street — right toward me.

The little kid yelled and started to cry, so when the older guy ran past me, I grabbed the bag, shoved him hard, and told him to go pick on someone his own size.

I splashed down to the BK parking lot and handed the little kid his pillowcase. He pushed his mask onto the top of his head and stared up at me, like he wasn't sure if I was going to help him or hit him. I knew I should probably say something wise to him, but all I could think of was "Hey, hold on to your bag tight so no one will steal it. And you shouldn't be out here alone at night. Where's your mom?"

He pointed across a busy street. I said, "Didn't she come with you?" He shook his head no, and there was nothing I could say to that, because my mom never took me trick-or-treating neither. I turned to walk away, when he said, "Here, mister." He reached in his bag and handed me a great big Hershey bar. With almonds. Little kids are cool, the way they look up to you and call you mister. And I thought it was *very* cool that he gave me a big candy bar, and not one of those little ones they call "fun size" but everyone knows just means tiny.

I watched that kid until he got down to the corner, lifting his bag over puddles and pushing up his clown mask so it wouldn't slide down his face. Why are moms always like that, sending their kids out alone in the dark?

A few minutes later, I stood inside Mr. Diggs's doorway, letting my eyes adjust to the darkness. Then I waited a second more, to adjust to seeing Mr. Diggs lying there in bed. He always looked worse. Always. Like somebody let a little more air out of him every day. He was deflating — getting more shrunk each time I saw him. He never said anything while I stood there adjusting, but I could tell he knew I was there. I finally said, "Hey, Willie Diggs, how you doing?"

He just reached around on his bed, trying to find the newspaper.

I said, "Today's Halloween. Wanna hear a ghost story instead of that newspaper?"

"No."

"I got a great big Hershey bar in my pocket," I said. "I took it from some little trick-or-treater on the street."

"Here's the newspaper." He held it out toward me.

"I really didn't steal the candy, you know. The kid gave it to me."

He didn't say anything.

"He gave it to me because I stopped another dude from ripping off his trick-or-treats. I chased the dude three blocks until he hopped a fence into a used car lot that had three German shepherd guard dogs. I left him there, hanging from the fence with the dogs chewing on his shoes."

When I pulled the brown paper from his *Detroit Free Press*, raindrops flew off my army jacket and splashed his face. "Hey!" he said angrily.

"Aw, calm down," I said. "It's just rain."

He reached up to touch his cheeks, and then just lay there for a minute with his hands on his face.

I said, "What's wrong?"

"I forgot how rain feels."

It was the first time he ever said anything to me that didn't sound mean or angry. He almost sounded sad. I said, "Wet. It feels wet."

Outside, the rain was tapping on the window like a thousand fingertips, so I went over and pulled up the shade. I brushed the dirt and dead bugs off the sill, then pried up the nails with the blade of my pocketknife. When I yanked open the window, the blind began clacking and cold wind and rain came rushing in. The raindrops splashed across the windowsill and bedside table, then sprinkled down on Mr. Diggs's pillow. In just a second, the whole side of his face was wet with little dots of rain.

I heard him take a long, deep breath.

I said, "Is it blowing too much?"

He shook his head no.

"Are you getting too wet?"

He shook his head no again.

I guess that was the first time I ever really liked the old guy.

Most of the time his face looked like a frozen mask with a mean expression, but that night, with the rain blowing on him, he looked different — not mean, just old and sad. After a while I sat down beside the bed and started reading him the obits, then the news stories, and finally even the sports page and comics, though I knew my hour was up and I really didn't have to stay. The paper flapped around in the breeze, and sometimes got so wet that I had a hard time seeing it, but I kept reading.

When I finally stood up to leave, I heard a crackling noise, but this time it wasn't a rat. It was the Hershey bar in my pocket. I took it out and tossed it on his bed. "Hey, Mr. Diggs, you can have this candy bar. I don't want it."

He snatched it up, then stuffed it deep into his pajama pocket. Well, who could blame him for hiding it with people like B. Otis and Bert Czarnowiak around? Still, it made me mad that he didn't say anything. I wanted to pull one of those B. Otis routines on him. Saying in a snotty voice, "Thanks for opening the window, Major. Thanks for the Hershey, Major," and making him repeat it back to me.

But I wouldn't do that to him.

It wasn't cool, and he probably wouldn't say it after me anyway. Just because I always squawked B. Otis's lines back at her didn't mean he'd do the same for me. Really, he was a tough old dude. Tougher than me.

So I said, "See ya, Willie Diggs," and headed out the door. Halfway down the hallway, Bert Czarnowiak popped out of a room and said, "Sir, can you help me?" I looked over my shoulder to make sure he was talking to me. He'd never called me sir before; *nobody*'d ever called me sir before.

"Sure. What do you need?" I said.

"I've got to find my Jeannie," he said.

"Who's that?"

"My wife," he said. "My wife, Jeannie."

And then he started crying. Crying as loud and as wet as women do on TV soap operas. Tears poured out of his eyes, then got trapped in wrinkles and slid sideways off his face. Usually he was whistling and dancing around saying, "Hee-hee-hee," so this was freaking me out. I took a giant step backwards and said, "What's with you?"

"I got to find *Jeannie*," he said, that last word getting all high-pitched and drawn out.

"She's here?" I asked. "Where?"

"I don't know. I don't know!" I was beginning to get the idea that maybe B. Otis had slipped Bert the wrong kind of drugs.

"Come on, I'll take you back to your room," I said, thinking I could add the extra time to my community service card. "Follow me." I started down the hall, but when I looked back, he was still standing there, saying, "Jeannie."

I needed to get him moving but didn't know how. Some people would have grabbed him by the hand or put their arm around his shoulder. Life's a lot easier for people who touch each other. But I'm not one of them. Finally I bent down and took the end of his belt, tugging it in my direction. The belt was the same faded blue as his robe but looked a little chewed up. I hoped rats hadn't done it. "Come on, Bert. Let's go back to your room," I said, then kind of pulled him along behind me, like a dog on a leash.

But then he suddenly turned and started running in the other direction, and I was on the end of *his* leash, moving fast to catch up. When he'd spin around, staring at the doors on both sides of the hall, I'd spin around behind him, trying not to knock him over. I was getting dizzy, spinning and running down that hall with him as he shouted, "Where's my Jeannie?"

Hunched over, I was seeing things I never saw before, like the dark line that ran across the middle of the walls, from where people had dragged their hands. When I lifted my head, I noticed how many bulbs were burned out in the ceiling sockets — and how the ones that worked weren't all the same brightness, so everything seemed to fade in and out as we ran.

Finally we were at the end of the hallway, right outside the room he shared with Mr. Diggs. He must have recognized the place because he hurried through the door, saying, "Jeannie? Jeannie?"

The blue belt slid from my hands, burning my palms.

I stayed in the doorway so he couldn't run out of the room. He stood there in the darkness and started to cry again. "Where *is* she?" he moaned.

Mr. Diggs was sitting up in bed, facing Mr. Czarnowiak. I guess he didn't know I was there to help out, because he slowly got out of bed, even though he had a hard time doing it.

I always saw him lying under a bunch of covers, so it was a surprise to see he could stand up and creak across the floor. It was an even bigger surprise to see how thin he was. When he passed the bedside lamp, the dim light glowed through his thin pajamas and I could see his legs were like chicken bones. "There now, there now," he said quietly. "There now."

He felt his way across the floor, with one hand reaching out in front of him, until he got to Bert. Then he put his hand on Bert's shoulder and led him to his bed.

"Where's Jeannie?" Bert kept whispering, and Mr. Diggs said, "Now, you know she ain't here. You know that. Come on now, sit down."

Then Mr. Diggs sat down next to Bert, reached in his pocket, and pulled out the Hershey bar. He carefully broke it in half, handed Bert a piece, and the two old guys sat quietly side by side, eating the candy and not saying a word.

I turned away and took a few steps into the hall, where I leaned against the wall to catch my breath and stop my head from spinning. When I felt better, I stretched my shoulders and stood as tall as I could. All that hunching over had made my back hurt. My hands were still closed tight from where I'd held Bert's belt, so I pried them open and stretched them wide.

For a couple seconds there, I really did feel old. And even though I didn't want to die young like the judge said, I sure didn't want to get old, either. Not like Bert Czarnowiak. Not like Willie Diggs. Because I could see up close and personal that getting old really sucks.

Every time I left that place, I ran all the way home, jumping over hedges and slapping at branches with my fingertips.

"Hey, how you doing?" I said, holding out my card to B. Otis.

She slammed down her magazine and stared at me. "Oh, THERE you are!" she shouted. "I've been waiting for you." I could tell she was the maddest she'd ever been because she was smiling more than I'd ever seen her smile.

"What's wrong?"

"Did you open a window last night?"

"Yeah. So what?"

"We have a POLICY against open windows!" she said, waving the orange card in my face. "AND Mr. Czarnowiak ate some candy yesterday. He's a diabetic. His blood sugar went sky high!"

"Is he dead?" I asked.

"Of course not! But he's in the infirmary. Neither he nor Mr. Diggs would say where they got the sweets. Did you bring anything in here last night?" Well, Willie Diggs and Bert were obviously being very cool! They didn't get me in trouble for the candy, and I sure didn't see any reason to get myself in trouble, either.

She finally quit yelling at me, and I headed down the hallway. Ever since the night before, when he lay there with that rain on his face, I'd been feeling a lot better about Mr. Diggs. Yeah, he was always mean and ticked off about something, but then so was I. We actually had a lot in common. Maybe by the time I finished my job at the Middlegate Retirement Plaza, he'd even be talking to me. But that night when I walked in his room and said, "Hey, Willie Diggs, how you doing?" he didn't answer. It was just like always.

"Thanks for not telling on me about the Hershey," I said. "I didn't know it wasn't allowed."

I grabbed the newspaper from the bed and unwrapped it, then flipped through the pages till I found the obits. "B. Otis just nailed me for opening the window," I said. "But don't worry, she can't fire me. I work for the state."

Of course Mr. Diggs didn't look worried at all. He just lay there, with his usual angry expression. I started to read the obituaries.

I was halfway through the first column when he gasped.

I thought maybe he recognized the name of the person who died. But when I looked at him, he was holding his hand up in the air, as if to say, "Wait a second."

He gasped again and put his hand on his chest.

"Mr. Diggs —," I said.

Again, he put up his hand to say, "Wait a second."

Don't ask me how, but I knew right then the old man was dying. I started to freak out. Should I get B. Otis? I didn't know what she'd do except smile at him. What about the nurse who worked in the infirmary? Could she do anything for him? Could I?

His face was suddenly covered with little dots of water, but this time it was sweat and not raindrops. He looked at me then. He was still blind and everything, but he turned his head and pointed his eyes directly at mine. They reflected back the bedside lamp and the light from the hallway and, as I leaned closer, my own face staring into his.

And then he grabbed my hand.

I didn't yell or pull away, even though I felt like it. I never knew a dying person would be that strong, but he squeezed my hand so tight I thought my fingers would break.

He didn't look mad anymore, just scared.

But now *I* was mad. I was furious that everything was ending this way. It was happening too fast. I wanted to say, "Wait a second, Willie Diggs. Just wait. Don't go before you tell me why you like the *Detroit Free Press*. Don't go without telling me who you are or what you think. You can't do this yet. Just wait a second. Wait. Please."

His black hand and my white one were gripped together tight against the ratty blue blanket and we were both pulling as hard as we could, but neither one of us ever did say a word out loud. And even after it was all over, I just kept on holding his hand. I thought it would take maybe five minutes for a dead person to turn into a Popsicle, but I must have sat there for fifteen minutes or more and he still felt warm and almost alive. I knew I should do something, but didn't know what. In movies, people sometimes say a prayer when someone dies, but I didn't know any prayers and didn't believe in them anyway.

So for a long time, I just sat there with him in the dark.

I stood at the end of the hallway and blinked my eyes at the light. B. Otis was sitting in her usual spot, this time reading *Life* magazine. When I walked in, she stuck the magazine under a folder. I said, "I'll be back tomorrow night."

She smiled at me with hate.

"By the way," I said, "I know you never bother to check, but you should probably take a look at Mr. Diggs tonight."

"Why?" she asked, smiling. "Is there a problem?"

"Yeah. He's dead."

I kept walking across the lobby, then outside, where it was brighter than it ever was before. Someone had finally changed that burned-out lightbulb in front of the building. I wanted to run all the way home, but I couldn't move. I could only stand on the top step and watch a couple moths — a great big one and dumb little one, smashing themselves against the light. I could only stand there listening to the trash compactor over at the Burger King. Breathing that greasy Whopper smell. I could only stand there feeling incredibly ticked off. People shouldn't have to live like that. Old and forgotten about. Mad all the time, and dying in a dark room where almost nobody cares about them. Grabbing someone's hand like that.

Why did he do it? People aren't supposed to touch you unless you say they can! So he shouldn't have done that to me. When the time comes for me to die, whether I'm eighteen years old, or one hundred and eighteen, I sure won't grab someone's hand like that. No. Not me. Never.

I took a long, deep breath, then started running — down the steps, through dark streets, over sidewalks and lawns, dodging cars and jumping curbs. But no matter how fast I ran or how far I went, I could still feel his hand holding on to mine.

# Antaeus

## Borden Deal

I remember this one kid, T.J. his name was, from somewhere down South; his family had moved into our building. They'd come north with everything they owned piled into the backseat of an old car that you wouldn't expect could make the trip, with T. J. and his three younger sisters riding shakily atop the load of junk.

Our building was just like all the others there, with families crowded into a few rooms, and I guess there were twenty-five or thirty kids about my age in that one building. Of course, there were a few of us who formed a gang and ran together all the time after school, and I was the one who brought T.J. in and started the whole thing.

The building right next door to us was a factory where they made walking dolls. It was a low building with a flat, tarred roof that had a parapet all around it about head-high, and we'd found out a long time before that no one, not even the watchman, paid any attention to the roof because it was higher than any of the other buildings around. So my gang used the roof as a headquarters. We could get up there by crossing over to the fire escape from our own roof on a plank and then going on up. It was a secret place for us, where nobody else could go without our permission.

I remember the day I first took T.J. up there to meet the gang. He was a stocky, robust kid with a shock of white hair, nothing sissy about him except his voice — he talked different from any of us and you noticed it right away. But I liked him anyway, so I told him to come on up.

We climbed up over the parapet and dropped down on the roof. The rest of the gang were already there.

"Hi," I said. I jerked my thumb at T.J. "He just moved into the building yesterday."

He just stood there, not scared or anything, just looking, like the first time you see somebody you're not sure you're going to like.

"Hi," Blackie said. "Where you from?"

"Marion County," T.J. said.

We laughed. "Marion County?" I said. "Where's that?"

He looked at me like I was a stranger too. "It's in Alabama," he said, like I ought to know where it was.

"What's your name?" Charley said.

"T.J.," he said, looking back at him. He had pale blue eyes that looked washed-out, but he looked directly at Charley, waiting for his reaction. He'll be all right, I thought. No sissy in him . . . except that voice. Who ever talked like that?

"T.J.," Blackie said. "That's just initials. What's your real name? Nobody in the world has just initials."

"I do," he said. "And they're T.J. That's all the name I got."

His voice was resolute with the knowledge of his rightness, and for a moment no one had anything to say. T.J. looked around at the rooftop and down at the black tar under his feet. "Down yonder where I come from," he said, "we played out in the woods. Don't you-all have no woods around here?"

"Naw," Blackie said. "There's a park a few blocks over, but it's full of kids and cops and old women. You can't do a thing."

T.J. kept looking at the tar under his feet. "You mean you ain't got no fields to raise nothing in? No watermelons or nothing?"

"Naw," I said scornfully. "What do you want to grow something for? The folks can buy everything they need at the store."

He looked at me again with that strange, unknowing look. "In Marion County," he said, "I had my own acre of cotton and my own acre of corn. It was mine to plant ever' year."

He sounded like it was something to be proud of, and in some obscure way it made the rest of us angry. "Heck!" Blackie said. "Who'd want to have their own acre of cotton and corn? That's just work. What can you do with an acre of cotton and corn?"

T.J. looked at him. "Well, you get part of the bale offen your acre," he said seriously. "And I fed my acre of corn to my calf."

We didn't really know what he was talking about, so we were more puzzled than angry; otherwise, I guess, we'd have chased him off the roof and wouldn't let him be part of our gang. But he was strange and different and we were all attracted by his stolid sense of rightness and belonging, maybe by the strange softness of his voice contrasting our own tones of speech into harshness.

He moved his foot against the black tar. "We could make our own field right here," he said softly, thoughtfully. "Come spring we could raise us what we want to . . . watermelons and garden truck and no telling what-all."

"You'd have to be a good farmer to make these tar roofs grow any watermelons," I said. We all laughed.

But T.J. looked serious. "We could haul us some dirt up here," he said. "And spread it out even and water it and before you know it, we'd have us a crop in here." He looked at us intently. "Wouldn't that be fun?"

"They wouldn't let us," Blackie said quickly.

"I thought you said this was you-all's roof," T.J. said to me. "That you-all could do anything you wanted up here."

"They've never bothered us," I said. I felt the idea beginning to catch fire in me. It was a big idea and it took a while for it to sink in but the more I thought about it the better I liked it. "Say," I said to the gang, "he might have something there. Just make us a regular roof garden, with flowers and grass and trees and everything. And all ours," I said. "We wouldn't let anybody up here except the ones we wanted to."

"It'd take a while to grow trees," T.J. said quickly, but we weren't paying any attention to him. They were all talking about it suddenly, all excited with the idea after I'd put it in a way they could catch hold of it. Only rich people had roof gardens, we knew, and the idea of our own private domain excited them.

"We could bring it up in sacks and boxes," Blackie said. "We'd have to do it while the folks weren't paying any attention to us. We'd have to come up to the roof of our building and then cross over with it."

"Where could we get the dirt?" someone said worriedly.

"Out of those vacant lots over close to school," Blackie said. "Nobody'd notice if we scraped it up."

I slapped T.J. on the shoulder. "Man, you had a wonderful idea," I said, and everybody grinned at him, remembering he had started it. "Our own private roof garden."

He grinned back. "It'll be ourn," he said. "All ourn." Then he looked thoughtful again. "Maybe I can lay my hands on some cotton seed too. You think we could raise us some cotton?"

We'd started big projects before at one time or another, like any gang of kids, but they'd always petered out for lack of organization and direction. But this one didn't. . . . Somehow or other T.J. kept it going all through the winter months. He kept talking about the watermelons and the cotton we'd raise, come spring, and when even that wouldn't work, he'd switch around to my idea of flowers and grass and trees, though he was always honest enough to add that it'd take a while to get any trees started. He always had it on his mind and he'd mention it in school, getting them lined up to carry dirt that afternoon, saying in a casual way that he reckoned a few more weeks ought to see the job through.

Our little area of private earth grew slowly. T.J. was smart enough to start in one corner of the building, heaping up the carried earth two or three feet thick, so that we had an immediate result to look at, to contemplate with awe. Some of the evenings T.J. alone was carrying earth up to the building, the rest of the gang distracted by other enterprises or interests, but T.J. kept plugging along on his own and eventually we'd all come back to him again and then our own little acre would grow more rapidly.

He was careful about the kind of dirt he'd let us carry up there, and more than once he dumped a sandy load over the parapet into the areaway below because it wasn't good enough. He found out the kinds of earth in all the vacant lots for blocks around. He'd pick it up and feel it and smell it, frozen though it was sometimes, and then he'd say it was good growing soil or it wasn't worth anything and we'd have to go on somewhere else.

Thinking about it now, I don't see how he kept us at it. It was hard work, lugging paper sacks and boxes of dirt all the way up the stairs of our own building, keeping out of the way of grown-ups so they wouldn't catch on to what we were doing. They probably wouldn't have cared, for they didn't pay much attention to us, but we wanted to keep it secret anyway. Then we had to go through the trapdoor to our roof, teeter over a plank to the fire escape, then climb two or three stories to the parapet and drop down onto the roof. All that for a small pile of earth that sometimes didn't seem worth the effort. But T.J. kept the vision bright within us, his words shrewd and calculated toward the fulfillment of his dream; and he worked harder than any of us. He seemed driven toward a goal that we couldn't see, a particular point in time that would be definitely marked by signs and wonders that only he could see.

The laborious earth just lay there during the cold months, inert and lifeless, the clods lumpy and cold under our feet when we walked over it. But one day it rained, and afterward there was a softness in the air and the earth was live and giving again with moisture and warmth. That evening T.J. smelled the air, his nostrils dilating with the odor of the earth under his feet.

"It's spring," he said, and there was a gladness rising in his voice that filled us all with the same feeling. "It's mighty late for it, but it's spring. I'd just about decided it wasn't never gonna get here at all."

We were all sniffing at the air, too, trying to smell it the way T.J. did, and I can still remember the sweet odor of the earth under our feet. It was the first time in my life that spring and spring earth had meant anything to me. I looked at T.J. then, knowing in a faint way the hunger within him through the toilsome winter months, knowing the dream that lay behind his plan. He was a new Antaeus, preparing his own bed of strength.

"Planting time," he said. "We'll have to find us some seed."

"What do we do?" Blackie said. "How do we do it?"

"First we'll have to break up the clods," T.J. said. "That won't be hard to do. Then we plant the seed and after a while they come up. Then you got a crop." He frowned. "But you ain't raised it yet. You got to tend it and hoe it and take care of it, and all the time it's growing and growing while you're awake and while you're asleep. Then you lay it by when it's growed and let it ripen and then you got you a crop."

"There's those wholesale seed houses over on Sixth," I said. "We could probably swipe some grass seed over there."

T.J. looked at the earth. "You-all seem mighty set on raising some grass," he said. "I ain't never put no effort into that. I spent all my life trying not to raise grass."

"But it's pretty," Blackie said. "We could play on it and take sunbaths on it. Like having our own lawn. Lots of people got lawns."

"Well," T.J. said. He looked at the rest of us, hesitant for the first time. He kept on looking at us for a moment. "I did have it in mind to raise some corn and vegetables. But we'll plant grass."

He was smart. He knew where to give in. And I don't suppose it made any difference to him really. He just wanted to grow something, even if it was grass.

"Of course," he said, "I do think we ought to plant a row of watermelons. They'd be mighty nice to eat while we was a-lying on that grass."

We all laughed. "All right," I said. "We'll plant us a row of watermelons."

Things went very quickly then. Perhaps half the roof was covered with the earth, the half that wasn't broken by ventilators, and we swiped pocketsful of grass seed from the open bins in the wholesale seed house, mingling among the buyers on Saturdays and during the school lunch hour. T.J. showed us how to prepare the earth, breaking up the clods and smoothing it and sowing the grass seed. It looked rich and black now with moisture, receiving of the seed, and it seemed that the grass sprang up overnight, pale green in the early spring.

We couldn't keep from looking at it, unable to believe that

we had created this delicate growth. We looked at T.J. with understanding now, knowing the fulfillment of the plan he carried alone within his mind. We had worked without full understanding of the task, but he had known all the time.

We found that we couldn't walk or play on the delicate blades, as we had expected to, but we didn't mind. It was enough just to look at it, to realize that it was the work of our own hands, and each evening the whole gang was there, trying to measure the growth that had been achieved that day.

One time a foot was placed on the plot of ground . . . one time only, Blackie stepping onto it with sudden bravado. Then he looked at the crushed blades, and there was shame in his face. He did not do it again. This was his grass, too, and not to be desecrated. No one said anything, for it was not necessary.

T.J. had reserved a small section for watermelons, and he was still trying to find some seed for it. The wholesale house didn't have any watermelon seed, and we didn't know where we could lay our hands on any. T.J. shaped the earth into mounds, ready to receive them, three mounds lying in a straight line along the edge of the grass plot.

We had just about decided that we'd have to buy the seed if we were to get them. It was a violation of our principles, but we were anxious to get the watermelons started. Somewhere or other, T.J. got his hands on a seed catalog and brought it one evening to our roof garden.

"We can order them now," he said, showing us the catalog. "Look!"

We all crowded around, looking at the fat, green watermelons pictured in full color on the pages. Some of them were split open, showing the red, tempting meat, making our mouths water.

"Now we got to scrape up some seed money," T.J. said, looking at us. "I got a quarter. How much you-all got?"

We made up a couple of dollars between us, and T.J. nodded his head. "That'll be more than enough. Now we got to decide what kind to get. I think them Kleckley Sweets. What do you-all think?"

He was going into esoteric matters beyond our reach. We hadn't even known there were different kinds of melons. So we just nodded our heads and agreed that yes, we thought the Kleckley Sweets too.

"I'll order them tonight," T.J. said. "We ought to have them in a few days."

Then an adult voice said behind us, "What are you boys doing up here?"

It startled us, for no one had ever come up here before, in all the time we had been using the roof of the factory. We jerked around and saw three men standing near the trapdoor at the other end of the roof. They weren't policemen, or night watchmen, but three plump men in business suits, looking at us. They walked toward us.

"What are you boys doing up here?" the one in the middle said again.

We stood still, guilt heavy among us, levied by the tone of voice, and looked at the three strangers.

The men stared at the grass flourishing behind us. "What's this?" the man said. "How did this get up here?"

"Sure is growing good, ain't it?" T.J. said conversationally. "We planted it."

The men kept looking at the grass as if they didn't believe it. It was a thick carpet over the earth now, a patch of deep greenness startling in the sterile industrial surroundings.

"Yes, sir," T.J. said proudly. "We toted that earth up here and planted that grass." He fluttered the seed catalog. "And we're just fixing to plant us some watermelon."

The man looked at him then, his eyes strange and faraway. "What do you mean, putting this on the roof of my building?" he said. "Do you want to go to jail?"

T.J. looked shaken. The rest of us were silent, frightened by the authority of his voice. We had grown up aware of adult authority, of policemen and night watchmen and teachers, and this man sounded like all the others. But it was a new thing to T.J.

"Well, you wan't using the roof," T.J. said. He paused a moment and added shrewdly, "so we thought to pretty it up a little bit."

"And sag it so I'd have to rebuild it," the man said sharply. He turned away, saying to a man beside him, "See that all that junk is shoveled off by tomorrow."

"Yes, sir," the man said.

T.J. started forward. "You can't do that," he said. "We toted it up here, and it's our earth. We planted it and raised it and toted it up here."

The man stared at him coldly. "But it's my building," he said. "It's to be shoveled off tomorrow."

"It's our earth," T.J. said desperately. "You ain't got no right!"

The man walked on without listening and descended clumsily through the trapdoor. T.J. stood looking after them, his body tense with anger, until they had disappeared. They wouldn't even argue with him, wouldn't let him defend his earth-rights.

He turned to us. "We won't let 'em do it," he said fiercely. "We'll stay up here all day tomorrow and the day after that and we won't let 'em do it."

We just looked at him. We knew that there was no stopping it. He saw it in our faces, and his face wavered for a moment before he gripped it into determination.

"They ain't got no right," he said. "It's our earth. It's our land. Can't nobody touch a man's own land."

We kept on looking at him, listening to the words but knowing that it was no use. The adult world had descended on us even in our richest dream, and we knew there was no calculating the adult world, no fighting it, no winning against it.

We started moving slowly toward the parapet and the fire escape, avoiding a last look at the green beauty of the earth that T.J. had planted for us . . . had planted deeply in our minds as well as in our experience. We filed slowly over the edge and down the steps to the plank, T.J. coming last, and all of us could feel the weight of his grief behind us.

"Wait a minute," he said suddenly, his voice harsh with the effort of calling. We stopped and turned, held by the tone of his voice, and looked up at him standing above us on the fire escape.

"We can't stop them?" he said, looking down at us, his face strange in the dusky light. "There ain't no way to stop 'em?"

"No," Blackie said with finality. "They own the building."

He stood still for a moment, looking up at T.J. caught into inaction by the decision working in his face. He stared back at us, and his face was pale and mean in the poor light, with a bald nakedness in his skin like cripples have sometimes.

"They ain't gonna touch my earth," he said fiercely. "They ain't gonna lay a hand on it! Come on."

He turned around and started up the fire escape again, almost running against the effort of climbing. We followed more slowly, not knowing what he intended. By the time we reached him, he had seized a board and thrust it into the soil, scooping it up and flinging it over the parapet into the areaway below. He straightened and looked us squarely in the face.

"They can't touch it," he said. "I won't let 'em lay a dirty hand on it!"

We saw it then. He stooped to his labor again and we followed, the gusts of his anger moving in frenzied labor among us as we scattered along the edge of earth, scooping it and throwing it over the parapet, destroying with anger the growth we had nurtured with such tender care. The soil carried so laboriously upward to the light and the sun cascaded swiftly into the dark areaway, the green glades of grass crumpled and twisted in the falling.

It took less time than you would think . . . the task of destruction is infinitely easier than that of creation. We stopped at the end, leaving only a scattering of loose soil, and when it was finally over, a stillness stood among the group and over the factory building. We looked down at the bare sterility of black tar, felt the harsh texture of it under the soles of our shoes, and the anger had gone out of us, leaving only a sore aching in our minds like overstretched muscles.

T.J. stooped for a moment, his breathing slowing from anger and effort, caught into the same contemplation of destruction as all of us. He stooped slowly, finally, and picked up a lonely blade of grass left trampled under our feet and put it between his teeth, tasting it, sucking the greenness out of it into his mouth. Then he started walking toward the fire escape, moving before any of us were ready to move, and disappeared over the edge while we stared after him.

We followed him, but he was already halfway down to the ground, going on past the board where we crossed over, climbing down into the areaway. We saw the last section swing down with his weight and then he stood on the concrete below us, looking at the small pile of anonymous earth scattered by our throwing. Then he walked across the place where we could see him and disappeared toward the street without glancing back, without looking up to see us watching him.

They did not find him for two weeks. Then the Nashville

police caught him just outside the Nashville freight yards. He was walking along the railroad track; still heading south, still heading home.

As for us, who had no remembered home to call us . . . none of us ever again climbed the escape-way to the roof.

# The Circuit

### Francisco Jiménez

It was that time of year again. Ito, the strawberry sharecropper, did not smile. It was natural. The peak of the strawberry season was over, and the last few days the workers, most of them *braceros,* were not picking as many boxes as they had during the months of June and July.

As the last days of August disappeared, so did the number of *braceros.* Sunday, only one — the best picker — came to work. I liked him. Sometimes we talked during our half-hour lunch break. That is how I found out he was from Jalisco, the same state in Mexico my family was from. That Sunday was the last time I saw him.

When the sun had tired and sunk behind the mountains, Ito signaled us that it was time to go home. "*Ya esora,*" he yelled in his broken Spanish. Those were the words I waited for twelve hours a day, every day, seven days a week, week after week. And the thought of not hearing them again saddened me.

As we drove home Papá did not say a word. With both hands on the wheel, he stared at the dirt road. My older brother, Roberto, was also silent. He leaned his head back and closed his eyes. Once in a while he cleared from his throat the dust that blew in from outside.

Yes, it was that time of year. When I opened the front door to the shack, I stopped. Everything we owned was neatly packed in cardboard boxes. Suddenly I felt even more the weight of hours, days, weeks, and months of work. I sat down on a box. The thought of having to move to Fresno and knowing what was in store for me there brought tears to my eyes.

That night I could not sleep. I lay in bed thinking about how much I hated this move.

A little before five o'clock in the morning, Papá woke everyone up. A few minutes later, the yelling and screaming of my little brothers and sisters, for whom the move was a great adventure, broke the silence of dawn. Shortly, the barking of the dogs accompanied them.

While we packed the breakfast dishes, Papá went outside to start the "Carcanchita." That was the name Papá gave his old black Plymouth. He bought it in a used-car lot in Santa Rosa. Papá was very proud of his little jalopy. He had a right to be proud of it. He spent a lot of time looking at other cars before buying this one. When he finally chose the Carcanchita, he checked it thoroughly before driving it out of the car lot. He examined every inch of the car. He listened to the motor, tilting his head from side to side like a parrot, trying to detect any noises that spelled car trouble. After being satisfied with the looks and sounds of the car, Papá then insisted on knowing who the original owner was. He never did find out from the car salesman, but he bought the car anyway. Papá figured the original owner must have been an important man because behind the rear seat of the car he found a blue necktie.

Papá parked the car out in front and left the motor running. "*Listo*," he yelled. Without saying a word, Roberto and I began to carry the boxes out to the car. Roberto carried the two big boxes and I carried the two smaller ones. Papá then threw the mattress on top of the car roof and tied it with ropes to the front and rear bumpers.

Everything was packed except Mamá's pot. It was an old large galvanized pot she had picked up at an army surplus store in Santa María the year I was born. The pot had many dents and nicks, and the more dents and nicks it acquired the more Mamá liked it. "*Mi olla*," she used to say proudly.

I held the front door open as Mamá carefully carried out her pot by both handles, making sure not to spill the cooked beans. When she got to the car, Papá reached out to help her with it. Roberto opened the rear car door and Papá gently placed it on the floor behind the front seat. All of us then climbed in. Papá sighed, wiped the sweat off his forehead with his sleeve, and said wearily, "*Es todo.*"

As we drove away, I felt a lump in my throat. I turned around and looked at our little shack for the last time.

At sunset we drove into a labor camp near Fresno. Since Papá did not speak English, Mamá asked the camp foreman if he needed any more workers. "We don't need no more," said the foreman, scratching his head. "Check with Sullivan down the road. Can't miss him. He lives in a big white house with a fence around it."

When we got there, Mamá walked up to the house. She went through a white gate, past a row of rosebushes, up the stairs to the front door. She rang the doorbell. The porch light went on and a tall husky man came out. They exchanged a few words. After the man went in, Mamá clasped her hands and hurried back to the car. "We have work! Mr. Sullivan said we can stay there the whole season," she said, gasping and pointing to an old garage near the stables.

The garage was worn out by the years. It had no windows. The walls, eaten by termites, strained to support the roof full of holes. The dirt floor, populated by earthworms, looked like a gray road map.

That night, by the light of a kerosene lamp, we unpacked and cleaned our new home. Roberto swept away the loose dirt, leaving the hard ground. Papá plugged the holes in the walls with old newspapers and tin can tops. Mamá fed my little brothers and sisters. Papá and Roberto then brought in the mattress and placed it on the far corner of the garage. "Mamá, you and the little ones sleep on the mattress. Roberto, Panchito, and I will sleep outside under the trees," Papá said.

Early next morning Mr. Sullivan showed us where his crop was, and after breakfast, Papá, Roberto, and I headed for the vineyard to pick.

Around nine o'clock the temperature had risen to almost one hundred degrees. I was completely soaked in sweat and my mouth felt as if I had been chewing on a handkerchief. I walked over to the end of the row, picked up the jug of water we had brought, and began drinking. "Don't drink too much; you'll get sick," Roberto shouted. No sooner had he said that than I felt sick to my stomach. I dropped to my knees and let the jug roll off my hands. I remained motionless with my eyes glued on the hot sandy ground. All I could hear was the drone of insects. Slowly I began to recover. I poured water over my face and neck and watched the dirty water run down my arms to the ground.

I still felt a little dizzy when we took a break to eat lunch. It was past two o'clock and we sat underneath a large walnut tree that was on the side of the road. While we ate, Papá jotted down the number of boxes we had picked. Roberto drew designs on the ground with a stick. Suddenly I noticed Papá's face turn pale as he looked down the road. "Here comes the school bus," he whispered loudly in alarm. Instinctively, Roberto and I ran and hid in the vineyards. We did not want to get in trouble for not going to school. The neatly dressed boys about my age got off. They carried books under their arms. After they crossed the street, the bus drove away. Roberto and I came out from hiding and joined Papá. "*Tienen que tener cuidado,*" he warned us.

After lunch we went back to work. The sun kept beating down. The buzzing insects, the wet sweat, and the hot dry dust made the afternoon seem to last forever. Finally the mountains around the valley reached out and swallowed the sun. Within an hour it was too dark to continue picking. The vines blanketed the grapes, making it difficult to see the bunches. "*Vámonos,*" said Papá, signaling to us that it was time to quit work. Papá then took out a pencil and began to figure out how much we had earned our first day. He wrote down numbers, crossed some out, wrote down some more. "*Quince,*" he murmured.

When we arrived home, we took a cold shower underneath a water hose. We then sat down to eat dinner around some wooden crates that served as a table. Mamá had cooked a special meal for us. We had rice and tortillas with *carne con chile,* my favorite dish.

The next morning I could hardly move. My body ached all over. I felt little control over my arms and legs. This feeling went on every morning for days until my muscles finally got used to the work.

It was Monday, the first week of November. The grape season was over and I could now go to school. I woke up early that morning and lay in bed, looking at the stars and savoring the thought of not going to work and of starting sixth grade for the first time that year. Since I could not sleep, I decided to get up and join Papá and Roberto at breakfast. I sat at the table across from Roberto, but I kept my head down. I did not want to look up and face him. I knew he was sad. He was not going to school today. He was not going tomorrow, or next week, or next month. He would not go until the cotton season was over, and that was sometime in February. I rubbed my hands together and watched the dry, acid-stained skin fall to the floor in little rolls.

When Papá and Roberto left for work, I felt relief. I walked to the top of a small grade next to the shack and watched the Carcanchita disappear in the distance in a cloud of dust.

Two hours later, around eight o'clock, I stood by the side of the road waiting for school bus number twenty. When it arrived I climbed in. Everyone was busy either talking or yelling. I sat in an empty seat in the back.

When the bus stopped in front of the school, I felt very nervous. I looked out the bus window and saw boys and girls carrying books under their arms. I put my hands in my pant pockets and walked to the principal's office. When I entered I heard a woman's voice say, "May I help you?" I was startled. I had not heard English for months. For a few seconds I remained speechless. I looked at the lady who waited for an answer. My first instinct was to answer her in Spanish, but I held back. Finally, after struggling for English words, I managed to tell her that I wanted to enroll in the sixth grade. After answering many questions, I was led to the classroom.

Mr. Lema, the sixth grade teacher, greeted me and assigned me a desk. He then introduced me to the class. I was so nervous and scared at that moment when everyone's eyes were on me that I wished I were with Papá and Roberto picking cotton. After taking roll, Mr. Lema gave the class the assignment for the first hour. "The first thing we have to do this morning is finish reading the story we began yesterday," he said enthusiastically. He walked up to me, handed me an English book, and asked me to read. "We are on page 125," he said politely. When I heard this, I felt my blood rush to my head; I felt dizzy. "Would you like to read?" he asked hesitantly. I opened the book to page

125. My mouth was dry. My eyes began to water. I could not begin. "You can read later," Mr. Lema said understandingly.

For the rest of the reading period I kept getting angrier and angrier with myself. I should have read, I thought to myself.

During recess I went into the restroom and opened my English book to page 125. I began to read in a low voice, pretending I was in class. There were many words I did not know. I closed the book and headed back to the classroom.

Mr. Lema was sitting at his desk correcting papers. When I entered he looked up at me and smiled. I felt better. I walked up to him and asked if he could help me with the new words. "Gladly," he said.

The rest of the month I spent my lunch hours working on English with Mr. Lema, my best friend at school.

One Friday during lunch hour Mr. Lema asked me to take a walk with him to the music room. "Do you like music?" he asked me as we entered the building.

"Yes, I like *corridos*," I answered. He then picked up a trumpet, blew on it, and handed it to me. The sound gave me goose bumps. I knew that sound. I had heard it in many *corridos*. "How would you like to learn how to play it?" he asked. He must have read my face because before I could answer, he added, "I'll teach you how to play it during our lunch hours."

That day I could hardly wait to get home to tell Papá and Mamá the great news. As I got off the bus, my little brothers and sisters ran up to meet me. They were yelling and screaming. I thought they were happy to see me, but when I opened the door to our shack, I saw that everything we owned was neatly packed in cardboard boxes.

# Glossary of Spanish Terms
## in "The Circuit"

*braceros:* day laborers

*Ya esora:* (*Ya es hora*) It's time

*Papá:* Father

*listo:* ready

*Mamá:* Mother

*mi olla:* my pot

*Es todo:* That's all

*Tienen que tener cuidado:* You have to be careful

*Vámonos:* Let's go

*quince:* fifteen

*carne con chile:* meat with chili

*corridos:* ballads

# Hollywood and the Pits

Cherylene Lee

When I was fifteen, the pit opened its secret to me. I breathed, ate, slept, dreamed about the La Brea Tar Pits. I spent summer days working the archaeological dig, and in dreams saw the bones glistening, the broken pelvises, the skulls, the vertebrae looped like a woman's pearls hanging on an invisible cord. I welcomed those dreams. I wanted to know where the next skeleton was, identify it, record its position, discover whether it was whole or not. I wanted to know where to dig in the coarse, black, gooey sand. I lost myself there and found something else.

My mother thought something was wrong with me. Was it good for a teenager to be fascinated by death? Especially animal death in the Pleistocene? Was it normal to be so obsessed by a sticky brown hole in the ground in the center of Los Angeles? I don't know if it was normal or not, but it seemed perfectly logical to me. After all, I grew up in Hollywood, a place where dreams and nightmares can often take the same shape. What else would a child actor do?

"Thank you very much, dear. We'll be letting you know."

I knew what that meant. It meant I would never hear from

them again. I didn't get the job. I heard that phrase a lot that year.

I walked out of the plush office, leaving behind the casting director, producer, director, writer, and whoever else came to listen to my reading for a semiregular role on a family sitcom. The carpet made no sound when I opened and shut the door.

I passed the other girls waiting in the reception room, each poring over her script. The mothers were waiting in a separate room, chattering about their daughters' latest commercials, interviews, callbacks, jobs. It sounded like every Oriental kid in Hollywood was working except me.

My mother used to have a lot to say in those waiting rooms. Ever since I was three, when I started at the Meglin Kiddie Dance Studio, I was dubbed "The Chinese Shirley Temple" — always the one to be picked at auditions and interviews, always the one to get the speaking lines, always called "the one-shot kid," because I could do my scenes in one take — even tight close-ups. My mother would only talk about me behind my back because she didn't want me to hear her brag, but I knew that she was proud. In a way I was proud too, though I never dared admit it. I didn't want to be called a show-off. But I didn't exactly know what I did to be proud of either. I only knew that at fifteen I was now being passed over at all these interviews when before I would be chosen.

My mother looked at my face hopefully when I came into the room. I gave her a quick shake of the head. She looked bewildered. I felt bad for my mother then. How could I explain it to her? I didn't understand it myself. We left, saying polite good-byes to all the other mothers.

We didn't say anything until the studio parking lot, where we had to search for our old blue Chevy among rows and rows of parked cars baking in the Hollywood heat.

"How did it go? Did you read clearly? Did you tell them you're available?"

"I don't think they care if I'm available or not, Ma."

"Didn't you read well? Did you remember to look up so they could see your eyes? Did they ask you if you could play the piano? Did you tell them you could learn?"

The barrage of questions stopped when we finally spotted our car. I didn't answer her. My mother asked about the piano because I lost out in an audition once to a Chinese girl who already knew how to play.

My mother took off the towel that shielded the steering wheel from the heat. "You're getting to be such a big girl," she said, starting the car in neutral. "But don't worry, there's always next time. You have what it takes. That's special." She put the car into forward and we drove through a parking lot that had an endless number of identical cars all facing the same direction. We drove back home in silence.

*In the La Brea Tar Pits many of the excavated bones belong to juvenile mammals. Thousands of years ago thirsty young animals in the area were drawn to watering holes, not knowing they were traps. Those inviting pools had false bottoms made of sticky tar, which immobilized its victims and preserved their bones when they died. Innocence trapped by ignorance. The tar pits record that well.*

I suppose a lot of my getting into show business in the first place was a matter of luck — being in the right place at the right time. My sister, seven years older than me, was a member of the Meglin Kiddie Dance Studio long before I started lessons. Once during the annual recital held at the Shrine Auditorium, she was spotted by a Hollywood agent who handled only Oriental performers. The agent sent my sister out for a role in the *CBS Playhouse 90* television show *The Family Nobody Wanted*. The producer said she was too tall for the part. But true to my mother's training of always having a positive reply, my sister said to the producer, "But I have a younger sister . . ." which started my showbiz career at the tender age of three.

My sister and I were lucky. We enjoyed singing and dancing, we were natural hams, and our parents never discouraged us. In fact they were our biggest fans. My mother chauffeured us to all our dance lessons, lessons we begged to take. She drove us to interviews, took us to studios, went on location with us, drilled us on our lines, made sure we kept up our schoolwork and didn't sass back the tutors hired by studios to teach us for three hours a day. She never complained about being a stage mother. She said that we made her proud.

My father must have felt pride too, because he paid for a choreographer to put together our sister act: "The World-Famous Lee Sisters," fifteen minutes of song and dance, real vaudeville stuff. We joked about that a lot, "Yeah, the Lee Sisters — Ug-Lee and Home-Lee," but we definitely had a good time. So did our parents. Our father especially liked our getting booked into Las Vegas at the New Frontier Hotel on the Strip. He liked to gamble there, though he said the craps tables in that hotel were "cold," not like the casinos in downtown Las Vegas, where all the "hot" action took place.

In Las Vegas our sister act was part of a show called "Oriental Holiday." The show was about a Hollywood producer going to the Far East, finding undiscovered talent, and bringing it back to the U.S. We did two shows a night in the main showroom, one at eight and one at twelve, and on weekends a third show at two in the morning. It ran the entire summer, often to standing-room-only audiences — a thousand people a show.

Our sister act worked because of the age and height difference. My sister then was fourteen and nearly five foot two; I was seven and very small for my age — people thought we were cute. We had song-and-dance routines to old tunes like "Ma, He's Making Eyes at Me," "Together," and "I'm Following You," and my father hired a writer to adapt the lyrics to "I Enjoy Being a Girl," which came out "We Enjoy Being Chinese." We also told corny jokes, but the Las Vegas audience seemed to enjoy it. Here we were, two kids, staying up late and jumping around, and getting paid besides. To me the applause sometimes sounded like static, sometimes like distant waves. It always amazed me when people applauded. The owner of the hotel liked us so much, he invited us back to perform in shows for three summers in a row. That was before I grew too tall and the sister act didn't seem so cute anymore.

*Many of the skeletons in the tar pits are found incomplete — particularly the skeletons of the young, which have only soft cartilage connecting the bones. In life the soft tissue allows for growth, but in death it dissolves quickly. Thus the skeletons of young animals are more apt to be scattered, especially the vertebrae protecting the spinal cord. In the tar pits, the central ends of many vertebrae are found unconnected to any skeleton. Such bone fragments are shaped like valentines, disks that are slightly lobed — heart-shaped shields that have lost their connection to what they were meant to protect.*

I never felt my mother pushed me to do something I didn't want to do. But I always knew if something I did pleased her. She was generous with her praise, and I was sensitive when she withheld it. I didn't like to disappoint her.

I took to performing easily, and since I had started out so

young, making movies or doing shows didn't feel like anything special. It was a part of my childhood — like going to the dentist one morning or going to school the next. I didn't wonder if I wanted a particular role or wanted to be in a show or how I would feel if I didn't get in. Until I was fifteen, it never occurred to me that one day I wouldn't get parts or that I might not "have what it takes."

When I was younger, I got a lot of roles because I was so small for my age. When I was nine years old, I could pass for five or six. I was really short. I was always teased about it when I was in elementary school, but I didn't mind because my height got me movie jobs. I could read and memorize lines that actual five-year-olds couldn't. My mother told people she made me sleep in a drawer so I wouldn't grow any bigger.

But when I turned fifteen, it was as if my body, which hadn't grown for so many years, suddenly made up for lost time. I grew five inches in seven months. My mother was amazed. Even I couldn't get used to it. I kept knocking into things, my clothes didn't fit right, I felt awkward and clumsy when I moved. Dumb things that I had gotten away with, like paying children's prices at the movies instead of junior admission, I couldn't do anymore. I wasn't a shrimp or a small fry any longer. I was suddenly normal.

Before that summer my mother had always claimed she wanted me to be normal. She didn't want me to become spoiled by the attention I received when I was working at the studios. I still had chores to do at home, went to public school when I wasn't working, was punished severely when I behaved badly. She didn't want me to feel I was different just because I was in the movies. When I was eight, I was interviewed by a reporter who wanted to know if I thought I had a big head.

"Sure," I said.

"No, you don't," my mother interrupted, which was really unusual, because she generally never said anything. She wanted me to speak for myself.

I didn't understand the question. My sister had always made fun of my head. She said my body was too tiny for the weight — I looked like a walking Tootsie Pop. I thought the reporter was making the same observation.

"She better not get that way," my mother said fiercely. "She's not any different from anyone else. She's just lucky and small for her age."

The reporter turned to my mother, "Some parents push their children to act. The kids feel like they're used."

"I don't do that — I'm not that way," my mother told the reporter.

But when she was sitting silently in all those waiting rooms while I was being turned down for one job after another, I could almost feel her wanting to shout, "Use her. Use her. What is wrong with her? Doesn't she have it anymore?" I didn't know what I had had that I didn't seem to have anymore. My mother had told the reporter that I was like everyone else. But when my life was like everyone else's, why was she disappointed?

*The churning action of the La Brea Tar Pits makes interpreting the record of past events extremely difficult. The usual order of deposition — the oldest on the bottom, the youngest on the top — loses all meaning when some of the oldest fossils can be brought to the surface by the movement of natural gas. One must look for an undisturbed spot, a place untouched by the action of underground springs or natural gas or human interference. Complete skeletons become important, because they indicate areas of least disturbance. But such spots of calm are rare. Whole blocks of the tar pit can become displaced, making false sequences of the past, skewing the interpretation for what is the true order of nature.*

That year before my sixteenth birthday, my mother seemed to spend a lot of time looking through my old scrapbooks, staring at all the eight-by-ten glossies of the shows that I had done. In the summer we visited with my grandmother often, since I wasn't working and had lots of free time. I would go out to the garden to read or sunbathe, but I could hear my mother and grandmother talking.

"She was so cute back then. She worked with Gene Kelly when she was five years old. She was so smart for her age. I don't know what's wrong with her."

"She's fifteen."

"She's too young to be an ingenue and too old to be cute. The studios forget so quickly. By the time she's old enough to play an ingenue, they won't remember her."

"Does she have to work in the movies? Hand me the scissors."

My grandmother was making false eyelashes using the hair from her hairbrush. When she was young she had incredible hair. I saw an old photograph of her when it flowed beyond her waist like a cascading black waterfall. At seventy, her hair was still black as night, which made her few strands of silver look like shooting stars. But her hair had thinned greatly with age. It sometimes fell out in clumps. She wore it brushed back in a bun with a hairpiece for added fullness. My grandmother had always been proud of her hair, but once she started making false eyelashes from it, she wasn't proud of the way it looked anymore. She said she was proud of it now because it made her useful.

It was painstaking work — tying knots into strands of hair, then tying them together to form feathery little crescents. Her glamorous false eyelashes were much sought after. Theatrical makeup artists waited months for her work. But my grandmother said what she liked was that she was doing something, making a contribution, and besides it didn't cost her anything. No overhead. "Till I go bald," she often joked.

She tried to teach me her art that summer, but for some reason strands of my hair wouldn't stay tied in knots.

"Too springy," my grandmother said. "Your hair is still too young." And because I was frustrated then, frustrated with everything about my life, she added, "You have to wait until your hair falls out, like mine. Something to look forward to, eh?" She had laughed and patted my hand.

My mother was going on and on about my lack of work, what might be wrong, that something she couldn't quite put her finger on. I heard my grandmother reply, but I didn't catch it all: "Movies are just make-believe, not real life. Like what I make with my hair that falls out — false. False eyelashes. Not meant to last."

*The remains in the La Brea Tar Pits are mostly of carnivorous animals. Very few herbivores are found — the ratio is five to one, a perversion of the natural food chain. The ratio is easy to explain. Thousands of years ago a thirsty animal sought a drink from the pools of water only to find itself trapped by the bottom, gooey with subterranean oil. A shriek of agony from the trapped victim drew flesh-eating predators, which were then trapped themselves by the very same ooze which provided the bait. The cycle repeated itself countless times. The number of victims grew, lured by the image of easy food, the deception of an easy kill. The animals piled on top of one another. For over ten thousand years the promise of the place drew animals of all sorts, mostly predators and scavengers — dire wolves, panthers, coyotes, vultures — all hungry for their chance. Most were sucked down against their will in those watering holes destined to be called the La Brea Tar Pits in a place to be named the City of Angels, home of Hollywood movie stars.*

I spent a lot of time by myself that summer, wondering what it was that I didn't have anymore. Could I get it back? How could I if I didn't know what it was?

That's when I discovered the La Brea Tar Pits. Hidden behind the County Art Museum on trendy Wilshire Boulevard, I found a job that didn't require me to be small or cute for my age. I didn't have to audition. No one said, "Thank you very much, we'll call you." Or if they did, they meant it. I volunteered my time one afternoon, and my fascination stuck — like tar on the bones of a saber-toothed tiger.

My mother didn't understand what had changed me. I didn't understand it myself. But I liked going to the La Brea Tar Pits. It meant I could get really messy and I was doing it with a purpose. I didn't feel awkward there. I could wear old stained pants. I could wear T-shirts with holes in them. I could wear disgustingly filthy sneakers and it was all perfectly justified. It wasn't a costume for a role in a film or a part in a TV sitcom. My mother didn't mind my dressing like that when she knew I was off to the pits. That was okay so long as I didn't track tar back into the house. I started going to the pits every day, and my mother wondered why. She couldn't believe I would rather be groveling in tar than going on auditions or interviews.

While my mother wasn't proud of the La Brea Tar Pits (she didn't know or care what a fossil was), she didn't discourage me either. She drove me there, the same way she used to drive me to the studios.

"Wouldn't you rather be doing a show in Las Vegas than scrambling around in a pit?" she asked.

"I'm not in a show in Las Vegas, Ma. The Lee Sisters are

retired." My older sister had married and was starting a family of her own.

"But if you could choose between . . ."

"There isn't a choice."

"You really like this tar-pit stuff, or are you just waiting until you can get real work in the movies?"

I didn't answer.

My mother sighed. "You could do it if you wanted, if you really wanted. You still have what it takes."

I didn't know about that. But then, I couldn't explain what drew me to the tar pits either. Maybe it was the bones, finding out what they were, which animal they belonged to, imagining how they got there, how they fell into the trap. I wondered about that a lot.

*At the La Brea Tar Pits, everything dug out of the pit is saved — including the sticky sand that covered the bones through the ages. Each bucket of sand is washed, sieved, and examined for pollen grains, insect remains, any evidence of past life. Even the grain size is recorded — the percentage of silt to sand to gravel that reveals the history of deposition, erosion, and disturbance. No single fossil, no one observation, is significant enough to tell the entire story. All the evidence must be weighed before a semblance of truth emerges.*

The tar pits had their lessons. I was learning I had to work slowly, become observant, to concentrate. I learned about time in a way that I would never experience — not in hours, days, and months, but in thousands and thousands of years. I imagined what the past must have been like, envisioned Los Angeles as a sweeping basin, perhaps slightly colder and more humid, a time before people and studios arrived. The tar pits recorded a warming trend; the kinds of animals found there reflected the changing climate. The ones unadapted disappeared. No trace of their kind was found in the area. The ones adapted to warmer weather left a record of bones in the pit. Amid that collection of ancient skeletons, surrounded by evidence of death, I was finding a secret preserved over thousands and thousands of years. There was something cruel about natural selection and the survival of the fittest. Even those successful individuals that "had what it took" for adaptation still wound up in the pits.

I never found out if I had what it took, not the way my mother meant. But I did adapt to the truth: I wasn't a Chinese Shirley Temple any longer, cute and short for my age. I had grown up. Maybe not on a Hollywood movie set, but in the La Brea Tar Pits.

# Carmella, Adelina, and Florry

## Norma Fox Mazer

Mary Beth Lichtow                           Mr. Nalius
American History, 4th period                October 10

ASSIGNMENT: AN ORAL HISTORY NARRATIVE FROM THE PAST

COMMENT: My mother talked into our tape recorder about the time she worked in a factory. Then I typed up what she said. It was extremely interesting. Until I had this assignment, I never knew my mom had worked in a factory!

My other comment is that when I did research for my mother's Oral History Narrative from the Past, I was really surprised to find out that only 20% of workers in the United States belong to unions. We did a whole unit on unions, so it seems they're very important. But if 80% of workers don't belong to unions, *they* must be pretty important, too!

(P.S., Mr. Nalius, maybe we can do a unit on workers who aren't in unions? And if such terrible things still happen to them, as happened to my mother?)

## Norma Fox Mazer

My name is Zelda Sagan Lichtow. I guess that's the first thing you'd want to know. I'm married, I have three kids, Susan, Jeff, and Mary Beth, and I work outside our home as a paralegal for Joffrey and Bogardus, who are terrific lawyers and married to each other. I only mention that last bit because it points up the fantastic difference between *right now* and the time I'm going to tell you about, which is the year 1949. That year I was nineteen and had just finished my first year of college.

In those days you might, just might, meet a woman who was a lawyer (or a doctor or an engineer) now and then, but most of us went to college to become teachers or librarians or social workers. It's only occurred to me recently that I have a real interest in the law, which is one reason I'm working as a paralegal. To sort of test the water, find out if I want to go to law school. I don't want to get off the point of my story, but this is background that I think is reasonably important.

Another thing about those days is that if you had the smarts to go to college, and if you could get up the money, you generally *stayed* in college. Dropping out was pretty much unknown, and certainly dropping out and then going back the way a lot of kids do today. In general everything about those days was less flexible than it is now.

Anyway, that fall when I was supposed to go back to school, I instead went to work as a punch-press operator in a mica-insulating factory. Now, to explain how I happened to go from college student to factory worker when I was perfectly happy *being* a college student, I'll have to tell you something personal about a boy I met. Actually I don't see how I can tell this story *without* being personal. (Besides, the idea that history isn't personal is ridiculous. What else is history, except people?)

Okay, it was 1949. A few years after World War II, and just before the Korean War, and *long* before the Vietnam War. A lot less money around than there is now. That's what I meant about staying in college — lots of people were just too poor to get there. We were on the better-off side of poor. My father and mother had both worked all their lives. I mean my mother had worked *outside* the home, as well as *inside*. They had both come from poor families and each had left school early to help *their* families. Well, you can see why they didn't want us kids to do that, and they did everything possible to see that we all finished high school and went to college.

I knew all this, but, no, I wasn't rebelling when I dropped out to work in the factory. It was just that that summer, while I was working in Rader's Cut Rite Drugs, I met Eric. Yes, enter Eric! An older man! He was twenty-five, and I was, well, *dazzled* by him. Maybe you'll think this is funny, but I'd had only one real boyfriend up to then. My parents had been *very* strict with me while I was in high school and when I got to college, things weren't all that much different. Colleges back then looked at themselves as *in loco parentis* — taking the place of parents, and especially for girls.

I had to be in my dorm by ten every night and have my lights out by eleven. On weekends I was allowed to stay out till one o'clock, but I had to sign in when I came back. And if I wanted to go someplace for a weekend, say, I couldn't just go. I needed the permission of my house mother.

Oh, that was nothing! There were rules and rules for girls. I don't know if anybody ever wrote them down, but every girl knew these rules by heart, anyway. Such as: You speak in a low voice. You don't act smart around boys. Let the *man* take the lead. And don't, above all, *don't* have sex before you're married. That was the way to perdition. [Laughs] If you could follow all those rules, you were considered a "nice girl" who'd be married before the dangerous old age of twenty-two!

Well, of course we all wanted to be nice, but, Lord, it was

so hard! You just couldn't be yourself. A little for-instance — I loved wearing jeans. Wore them with the cuffs rolled up and with a big man's shirt tied at the waist. Well, that was all right for weekends, but for school — forget it! It had to be stockings and skirts and little strings of fake pearls. Ladylike, you know.

And if you were the least bit plump — and I was, for a while — under that skirt you wore a girdle. Oh! Just thinking of that girdle gives me the willies. A torture garment. As for your — What do you kids call them now? Your boobs — there wasn't a girl I knew, including me, who wasn't miserable about what she had. Either too much or too little, according to some mystical idea of perfection. I mean, *male* idea of perfection! We all felt such pressure to be perfect! And to catch a man! *That,* after all, was the big goal. Success in life. [Laughs]

Listen, every night I rolled my hair up on metal curlers and then slept on those hunks of metal. More torture. But, heavens, you couldn't go to school with straight hair! Everything really was so much more rigid and codified. That's what appealed to me about Eric.

To begin with, he looked like an Eric — beautiful, Nordic, Viking type. He'd been in the army, he'd been to college (on the GI Bill), and he'd done this absolutely incredible thing of getting a degree, and *then not using it*. From college, with his precious bachelor of arts degree, he'd become a bus driver!

Now this bus he was driving happened to stop right in front of Rader's Cut Rite Drugs at least four times every day. And he would come in, buy a candy bar, or a newspaper. You know. It wasn't long before we went from joking over the counter to going out on dates. Oh, I was just dazzled. Eric was different from any of the boys I knew. He had ambition, but it wasn't the ambition to be a professional and make boodles of money. His ambition was to be a union organizer. And more than that, he had *principles*. Socialist principles. He wanted to change society. Change people. Change the way things were done. I had never heard such ideas — the workers taking over the factories and having the profits, instead of the owners? And the words he used! Today, everyone uses words like *establishment, power structure,* and *the military-industrial complex.* But back then? I'd never heard things like that. Eric's very favorite word, though, was *bourgeois.*

I can still remember his saying to me, "Zel, your father is a worker, but *you* are bourgeois to your soul." It was the *worst* thing he could call anyone! It meant having middle-class values. Being concerned about things like getting a college degree and worrying about my appearance.

He was right about me. [Laughs] I was trying so hard to be nice, to get ahead, to do all these things. And what for? According to Eric, so I could leave the working class, which he spoke of as "noble" (as well as "exploited"), and become one of those people who lived a smug, self-satisfied life of materialistic values!

Furthermore, he said, when you got right down to it, the most bourgeois aspect of my behavior was my attitude about sex. To put it bluntly, Eric wanted to make love, and I was resisting. Naturally! I was a nice girl! Everything I'd been taught was that nice girls *didn't,* not until they got married.

I remember one day, after the usual push-pull, Eric blurting out, "You must think it's property. You act like an incipient capitalist, hoarding his stake. I guess," he said, "it's going to take you a lot longer to get rid of your false bourgeois attitudes."

I just didn't know what to say. I was crushed by his remarks. He sounded so reproachful, so regretful, so *sad.*

I'm sure that was the moment when I decided that if I couldn't live up to Eric's standards one way, I'd do it another way. I'd find a factory job and become one of the "oppressed masses" he revered.

My parents were stunned by my decision not to go back to school that fall. But I guess some things never change. When you're nineteen and think you're in love, you're not listening to your parents.

Anyway, the first place I tried, MIF, Mica Insulating Factory, hired me. Just like that. Couldn't believe it. Someone from personnel pointed me across a yard to the Women's Building and told me to find Eddy, the foreman, and give him my hiring slip.

The Women's Building was concrete with steel doors. I swear the walls actually quivered from the sound of what seemed to me to be a thousand presses. I found the foreman at the far end of this huge, noisy room near a stand-up desk. He took the hiring slip. "Your name is Zelda?" he shouted. I didn't like his eyes — they were like little dirty pebbles — and I didn't like the way he looked me over with those eyes.

"You fast?" he shouted. I nodded. "Not afraid to work?" He wrote something on a dirty yellow legal pad clipped to a dirty clipboard. Everything was dirty in that place — the floor, the walls, Eddy's fingernails, the windows, his desk.

Oh, I should qualify that. The women who worked there — they *sparkled*. They dressed like gypsies or dancers, with big hoop earrings, and scarves over their hair, and swirly skirts and bright blouses.

Anyway, Eddy gave me a shove and pointed me toward Florry on number-ten machine. Florry was English, she was redheaded, she was about my mother's age, and she was a great woman. I found her sitting like a queen in front of her machine, her back straight as a ruler. I stood and watched her for a moment. Her hands moved so beautifully, so fast, she was so perfectly coordinated with the machine that I knew I'd never be able to compare.

I tapped her on the shoulder and yelled that Eddy had sent me. "New girl?" she said. "Watch, now."

From a basket near her left foot she took a handful of mica fragments, dropped them on the machine counter, slipped one golden brown chip under the machine arm, and pressed a lever with her other foot. The huge heavy arm came down — *WHANG!* It was the sound of those machine arms, fifty of them, coming down second after second that filled the air with such a thick, deafening din.

The arm came down on the mica and a round disc with a serrated edge was stamped out. Florry moved the mica, down came the arm — she did that again and once more. Got four cuts out of that one piece. A little like cutting cookie dough. Only with cookie dough, if you press the cutter too close to the edge and don't make a perfect round, you can still bake the cookie. Here, you could keep only the perfect cuts, which were then pushed down a chute in back of the machine. The pieces you messed up went into a scrap basket. And you didn't make any money on them.

"That's it," Florry mouthed to me, after showing me the procedure a couple more times. "Go to it." She nodded to the empty machine next to hers.

I sat down on the iron stool, turned on the power, and watched the belt slipping around the arm. I was terrified as I slid the first piece of yellow mica under the arm and pressed the lever foot. *WHANG!* I had good reason to be scared. You could lose your fingers, with no trouble at all, to that arm. In fact, there were several three- and four-fingered women working in the building.

*WHANG! WHANG! WHANG!* My foot slipped and I punched the mica three times without moving it around. I'd ruined the piece. I looked around, afraid Eddy was watching. He was! My face burned; my hands were damp. Oh, I was sweating. Those first hours I must have lost five pounds just from anxiety.

At noon a whistle shrilled and the machines shut down. My head felt numb in the silence. Then the quiet was broken again, but this time by the more pleasant sounds of fifty women laughing and talking, rushing toward the time clock.

Florry caught my arm and pulled me into the mass of women carrying sweaters, newspapers, lunch bags, and Thermoses. "Come along, girl! Did you bring your lunch? Hurry now, luv. We don't have that much time. Twenty minutes."

As it turned out, more than enough for me. The moment Florry led me into the "lunchroom," I lost my appetite. Flaking vomit-green walls. Scabby-looking linoleum underfoot. And then the dandiest feature of the "ladies' lounge" — a flimsy, shoulder-high partition separating those eating lunch from those using the row of toilet stalls.

The room was packed. Women leaned against the walls, squeezed onto a cracked brown leather couch and a couple of chairs, squatted on the floor, and sat in each other's laps.

"Girls!" I noticed how everyone stopped talking to listen to Florry. "This is Zelda, the new girl on number nine."

"Hi, Zelda, welcome to the zoo."

"Zelda, cute name!"

"Think you're going to like it here?"

The calls and shouts came from all over. I smiled. "Hi! I guess it's going to be fun working here."

You should have heard them then. Catcalls, hoots, laughter, groans.

A toilet flushed and I asked Florry if you could eat outside. "Certainly, luv."

"Don't do it," someone said. "It makes you koo-koo."

"Aww, she'll go koo-koo just working here."

"You wanna try the prison yard, honey, you try it. It's great, ha ha."

"Whatsa matter? You don't like our ladies' lounge? This place is just like home, ain't it, girls?"

I smiled from one to the other. I didn't have them sorted out yet into names to go with faces.

"She's cute," someone said about me, "but she don't look old enough to even have her working papers." This made me blush. My round baby face was always embarrassing me.

"You got a boyfriend, Zelda?" That was Carmella, a skinny imp with a cloud of dark hair and eyes that danced mischievously behind thick lenses. She and I got friendly, but that day I just didn't know what to say when she went on, "Your boyfriend do you yet?" I blushed even harder.

"Aww, leave the nice baby alone." Then a loud happy laugh. And that was how I first picked Adelina out of the crowd. She was a little soft-looking woman with huge dark popping eyes. A sweetie pie. Her husband had left her, she was raising four kids alone, she'd lost a home to fire and one child to polio, but she had the biggest, freshest, loudest, happiest laugh I can ever remember hearing. When Adelina laughed — and all sorts of things struck her funny — it was irresistible.

It seemed I'd hardly found a corner of a chair to sit on, had hardly begun talking to Adelina and Carmella, when the whistle blew. Everyone rushed for the door, scrambling to be first at the time clock. "You get docked half an hour if you're more than five minutes late," Florry explained, pulling me along by the arm. "Hurry!"

Hurry! Hurry! Hurry! That was the pace of life in MIF. Wake up in the morning and hurry to work! Rush that mica through the machine! Got to make the rate! Hurry to the lunchroom! Hurry back! Get to work!

Every night I was exhausted, aching. I'd never worked like this in my life. My parents watched me and said little. I think, now, that they were just waiting for me to get over my romantic ideas about the glories of factory life.

As for Eric — couldn't have been more pleased! He was in his element, educating me, lecturing, pointing out to me that I had a unique opportunity. "These are the most downtrodden workers, Zelda. The unorganized. They are the most grossly exploited. You can help them understand that they can take their destinies into their own hands. They need to be organized."

I didn't disagree about that, but I didn't think I could educate anyone in that shop to anything. As for "downtrodden," that just made me laugh. Carmella? Adelina? Florry? *Downtrodden*? They worked twice as fast as I did, twice as hard, and they could still sing, scream jokes to each other, and notice every man who came into the shop.

Machines were always breaking down. "Number twenny-three down," someone would yell. A mechanic came running, and the bawdy remarks flew through the air.

"Oh, Lord, he's so sweet," Carmella caroled.

"Do you think he's taken?" From another side of the room.

"Come here and see *me*, honey. I'm sure something's wrong with my machine that *you* can fix."

And I just listened, laughing, blushing. They dubbed me "the baby." Why not? I was so naive. After working two weeks, my first paycheck thrilled me. "Look at all this money," I said to Carmella. "This is great."

"Ain't nothing great but loving," Carmella assured me, as if I were about twenty years younger than she was, instead of only two.

In fact, on Friday, when pay envelopes were opened, there was gloom in the lunchroom. Friday was the worst day of the week. Friday was when people found out if they made their piecework rate.

Here's how that worked. A price was put on each little piece stamped out on the press. It might be an eighth of a cent if the die, the pattern, was tiny, or as much as a penny if the die was large. The smallest dies paid the least because you could get the most cuts from a single piece of mica. So, the theory was, it was an advantage. Whip that piece around, get eight cuts, and make that penny just as fast as someone with a large penny die.

But, in fact, the eighth of a cent or the quarter of a cent was earned only on good cuts. And how you got good cuts depended on lots of things. To begin with — pray for Eddy to deliver you a load of mica neither too thick nor too brittle. Pray for your machine not to break down. Pray you could keep that machine *WHANG! WHANG! WHANG! WHANG! WHANGING!* as fast as it could go. Never think about the fingers that had been lost to the machine. Never slack off. And, on a good day, you might make as much as a dollar and a half an hour. If you could do that every day, then there'd be sixty dollars in the pay packet. That was a lot of money. A powerful lot of money! Everyone was always trying for the big sixty. But only a few of Eddy's pets ever made it.

For every good day when an operator made that kind of money, there were the other days when she made forty or fifty cents an hour. And on Friday, gloomy Friday, nearly everyone ended with a little more or a little less than forty dollars for forty hours of work.

A month passed. I was learning. No longer so glowing about facing that punch press every day. Amazed, abashed, to learn that Adelina had worked there for ten years, Carmella for four, Florry for five. And had no idea of ever working anywhere else.

"Well, well? Are you talking to them about the union?" Eric prodded me.

I mumbled something. He had such a — such a *false* idea of what I could do. What *could* I do? I was green, I was raw, I didn't know half what anyone else in that place knew about what it meant to work, to be underpaid, and still hold up your head.

Then, in a manner I could never have foreseen, I *did* have something to do with changing things in MIF. It was totally accidental.

I remember, one day, Carmella's asking me if Eddy had been bothering me. Well, he did hang around my machine a lot, but I thought he was just checking my work.

Carmella linked arms with me. "Watch out for him — he's got roaming hands."

"Oh, I can take care of myself," I said quickly. I certainly felt like a big well-fed horse next to skinny Carm.

She laughed at me. She knew me better than I knew me. "If he tries anything, you just tell him — " And she chopped her right hand into the crook of her left elbow.

A few nights later I showed Eric the arm salute, proud of everything I was learning, of my independence, of my new swaggering style — gypsy skirts, bright scarves around my hair, and big hoop earrings. I'd had my ears pierced. Carmella had done it in the lunchroom. Put an ice cube on my earlobe, held it there for a moment, then punched a needle through the lobe and left a silk thread in the hole.

"You've changed," Eric said. Did he sound a bit miffed? "I never thought you'd do it, you know. Go into the factory that way. And — " He looked at me, almost helplessly. "And *everything.*"

"I know. You thought I was too *bourgeois.*" I stuck out my tongue, like Angie, the new bride that everyone teased. And I gave him the arm salute again.

"You're really getting *sassy,*" he said.

Sure I was! It was the influence of my new friends, my new world. I felt as if my parents had been keeping a secret from me all these years. I'd always felt sorry for them, having to go to work in a factory every day. But now it turned out they must have been having fun, too.

One night Eric and I parked. We talked about the shop first — that was "business" — then got into our inevitable hassle over how far we were going to "go." "You're still so backward," he said at last, giving up. He frowned handsomely, smoking and looking out the window.

"I'm sorry," I said.

"I don't see much of you anymore, either," he complained.

"I know. I'm sorry. I'm so tired at night." Why did I keep saying to him that I was sorry? Sorry I couldn't make love. Sorry I wasn't on call. Sorry I was so ignorant. Sorry I hadn't already converted everyone in MIF to union thoughts. I made up my mind that before I said "sorry" once more to Eric, I'd sooner cut out my tongue.

So there we sat, Eric sulking, me silent. I kept staring at his wonderful Viking profile. It didn't seem to matter so much, anymore, that he was so attractive. The truth was, I realized, I thought more about the women I worked with than I did about him. And then I surprised myself again by thinking that I loved my shop friends more, *much more,* than Eric. Now *that* was a revolutionary thought. Don't forget, the general idea then was that the company of any man (not even to speak of an exceptional one like Eric) was infinitely preferable to the company of *any* woman, no matter how interesting or lively. Oh, yeah? [Laughs] Wanna bet?

Well, a few days later, I was a little slow leaving my machine at lunchtime. I was mulling over Eric and where we were headed. Before I knew it, the room had emptied, Eddy loomed up, and yes, indeed, he did have roaming hands. I know it's a cliché, but my heart was pounding so hard with shock, I really thought it was going to break through my chest. I don't know if I said anything to him, pushed him away, or just ran for my life.

The next thing I remember is bursting into the lunchroom, and little fat Mary Margaret, with her mouth full of food, saying, "Look at Zelda, look at Zelda, her face is all red."

Everyone stopped talking and looked at me.

"What happened, baby?" Adelina asked me in her husky voice.

"Eddy — ," I gulped. All I could get out was his name. Didn't want to cry, but the tears flowed anyway.

"Eddy, huh!" Carmella patted my back.

Everyone seemed to know without another word what it meant.

"Gee, don't cry," Mary Margaret said. "We all been felt up when we didn't wanna be."

That made me cry harder. And, with that, Angie, our bride, put her apron over her face and started to cry, too! It seemed that the day before, when she was at her machine, Eddy had put his hand up her skirt.

"Men! They're all alike," Adelina said hoarsely. "But that Eddy is a real dog," she added.

"He's got no right," Angie bawled. "I didn't give him the right."

"Girls!" Florry sat up straight. "It's a bloody shame when kids like Angie and Zelda can't do a day's work without being molested." Her voice rose over Angie's bawling. "We don't belong to Eddy. We don't belong to the company. Just because we work here, break our backs for pennies!"

"Ain't it the truth," someone sighed.

Florry's head snapped around. "Isn't it bloody disgusting what we work for? Isn't it bloody disgusting that we have to eat in this little pokehole?"

There were murmurs around the room. Agreement or disagreement? I couldn't tell. My tears had dried up.

Florry stood up, put her hands on hips, and turned to look at each and every woman. When she had our attention, she said slowly, "Let's do something for ourselves, *for once*. Stick together, *for once*."

"What can we do?" a voice bleated.

Just then the whistle blew. There was the usual stirring, women standing, smoothing their hair, crumpling lunch bags. "Girls!" Florry raised her voice. "Why don't we *sit right here* until bloody Eddy bloody promises to keep his hands to himself!"

"You mean not go back to our machines?" Mary Margaret squeaked. "Not go back to *work?*"

"That's what I mean."

For a moment the room went quiet with shock. Then came the protests, a hubbub of sound. "We can't do that!" "They'll *fire* us." "I need my job."

"Fire us?" Florry sniffed scornfully. "There are thirty-bloody-three of us here! They're not going to fire thirty-three operators. Girls, do we or don't we have backbone?"

Someone crunched an apple. A toilet flushed. And everyone looked at everyone else. Then the door burst open. Not even a knock, and Eddy was inside, pulling at his greasy hair, screaming. "What the hell is going on? You girls know what time it is?" He showed his yellow teeth in a snarl. "Get back to work!"

Carmella jumped up, crossing her matchstick arms, skinny elbows sticking out. "Why don't you keep your paws to yourself," she screeched. "We know what you did to Zelda and Angie."

"Shut up, you! Now, haul ass back to them machines, or you're all fired." He grabbed Carmella, who was half his size, and started dragging her toward the door. That was a mistake.

Adelina rushed to Carmella's rescue. Then Florry. In another moment Eddy was surrounded by women screaming at him and dragging poor Carm away. A wonder her arms weren't broken.

"You creep!" I could hear Adelina's husky voice over everyone else's. "You Jack the Ripper!" Her eyes were nearly popping out of her head. "You dirty old thing." Then the clincher. "What'samatter, brother, you can't get it at home?" And she gave one of her loud, joyous laughs.

Eddy turned brick-red. "I give you five minutes," he yelled over the pandemonium, "or the whole bunch of you is out on the sidewalk." He slammed out.

Well, then the *silence*. Like they say, you could have cut it with a knife. Adelina collapsed into a chair with a deep, sad sigh. After a bit she said, "Well, we had our fun, so now let's forget it. You girls know I got to support my kids. I can't afford to lose my job. None of us can."

Three or four women slipped out. There was a general stir. Carmella nursed her bruised arm. "Girls," Florry said quietly, "if we give in now, Eddy will be worse than ever. He'll know we're scared of him. I'm ready to sit. Is anyone else?"

Silence again. And again everyone looked at everyone else. Waiting for the other person to make the first move one way or the other, to say the first word. Then, of all people, little fat Mary Margaret, looking half scared to death, stood up, said, "I'll do it!" and collapsed back into her seat, pudgy hands clasped at her heart.

We all stared at Mary Margaret, who, up till that moment, had made her chief claim to fame on eating three bananas every day for lunch. Adelina whistled through her teeth. Carmella gave a raucous laugh. "Hey! I ain't gonna be shamed by Mary. I'll stay, too." She swaggered over to the couch.

Another few women left. Florry, like an avenging redheaded

goddess, once again looked eye-to-eye with each woman. I could feel the tension, the nervousness, in the air, like strings being drawn across my skin. Were we going to stay? Or were we going to give in to Eddy?

Reve Fernmaker, a big motherly woman, tucked her gray hair back into its bun and cleared her throat. Heads swiveled. "Well," Reve said comfortably, "I need my job, too." She smoothed her apron. "But — I'm for staying."

A deep sigh seemed to pass around the room, from woman to woman. Without another word of discussion everyone settled down. "What now?" Francie said. She was a pretty girl with a little cupid's-bow mouth. Wore a whole lot of makeup, and supported herself and her boyfriend with her job at MIF and yodeling on weekends in bars. "What happens now?"

The same question we all had.

What happened was that fifteen minutes later Eddy was back. "Move, you pigs! Get to them machines!"

My God, I've never seen anyone so furious in my life. I thought he'd have a stroke on the spot. His face was boiling, twice its normal size. "Move!" He was screaming, out of control.

"We ain't moving," Adelina said. "We want some changes around here."

"We — ain't — moving!" Francie, the yodeler, chanted it, softly clapping her hands. And everyone took it up.

"We ain't moving! We ain't moving! We ain't moving!" We pounded our feet on the floor. "We ain't moving!"

We sat in the lunchroom all afternoon, talking and singing. Francie yodeled for us, did her nightclub act, and we all applauded, stamped, and whistled. I remember we sang popular songs, too, especially "Riders in the Sky." Everyone was singing that one, that year. It was Vaughn Monroe's big hit.

And every time Eddy stuck his head in the door and

screamed at us pigs to get back to them machines, we laughed in his face. I remember Carmella saying, "How come we dopes didn't ever do this sooner?"

One time when Eddy came in, Reve, the motherly one, went nose-to-nose with him and said very quietly, "And don't you call us 'girls' in that tone of voice, mister. We are *women*. We are grown-up women, and we demand some *respect*." It was a wonderful moment. I still get chills down my back, remembering.

Around four o'clock the company supervisor appeared. One of the big shots and quite a different person from Eddy. A handsome, silvery-haired man wearing a sweater and a tie. Very relaxed, easy, sympathetic. He listened to the complaints Florry listed, nodding, giving warm, fatherly looks. Florry spoke about the rates, Eddy's roaming hands, and the ugliness of our lunchroom.

"I don't blame you ladies for being upset," he said. He made promises. A new lunchroom, longer lunch hour, and as for Eddy, he said flatly, "You won't have any trouble with him again."

When he left, we all did, too. We thought we had won. Eddy watched us go, stood there saying nothing, his hands in his pockets. After all the exhilaration, all the emotion, the singing and shouting, we left quietly, arms around each other. I felt wonderful — powerful, maybe, for the first time in my life.

The very next day, the lunchroom was painted a sunny yellow. Two days later three new chairs appeared. "You see what happens when we stick together," Florry said. And Carmella said, "Ain't it the truth!" Then, on Friday, when we got our pay packets, Eddy told Adelina, Carmella, Florry, and me not to bother coming back. Fired. All of us, fired for being troublemakers.

Everyone watched us leave. Everyone knew about the firings. That was the point — to scare all the other women into being "good" again. Florry was just sick about how we'd been taken in by the company supervisor. "That bloody smooth-talking bloody man!" Adelina was pretty upset, too, afraid she wouldn't find another job.

Well, all of us managed to find work. We kept in touch the next few months. I went to work in a box factory, putting together cardboard boxes. [Laughs] Someone has to do that, you know. And then I had a job sewing baseballs and, for a short while, I worked as a chambermaid in a hotel. It was never the same as working in MIF, though. Never the same as working with Florry, Carmella, and Adelina.

By the time fall rolled around, I was ready to go back to school. And I did. And — you know how these things are — I didn't forget my friends, but now our lives were so different.

Well, over winter vacation I was home, and I ran into Mary Margaret. We went into a White Tower and had hamburgers, and she told me that right after the firings there'd been talk about getting in the union. But it died down when the company promised to review the piecework rate, to increase paid holidays, and give ten days a year sick leave.

In fact, though, it was all talk. Nothing had changed. Everything was back to "normal." Except now, a lot of women were for the union — they realized that without a union they had no power whatsoever. But no one dared come out in the open and say this. Not if they wanted to keep their jobs.

After that I didn't hear anything for a couple more years. Then the strangest coincidence — the same month I graduated from college my mother sent me news that there had been (for the second time) an NLRB election in the plant, and this time the union had won. I burst into tears. I remember exactly how I felt, what I thought. *At last! At last. A victory for the girls.*

So, that's pretty much the end of the story. Oh, one other point I was thinking about as I was telling you all this. You notice how we called ourselves and each other "girls"? And remember when Reve Fernmaker stood up to Eddy and told him we were *women*? I don't think there's really any contradiction there.

We didn't say "sisters" then, the way some women do today. But I think calling each other "girls" was a kind of substitute for that. Sometimes it was ironic. Sometimes affectionate. But, always, there was all the difference in the world between the way *we* said it to one another, and the way Eddy or any other man said it to *us*.

Well, that really is the end of my story. Unless you want to know about Eric and me. That's history, too, isn't it? Even if, of a lesser kind. What happened was — we just saw less and less of each other. No longer found each other so interesting. I wonder if Eric even remembers me anymore. I can just see him wrinkling his handsome brow and saying, "Zelda Sagan? Zelda Sagan? Hmm. . . ." [Laughs] Of course I've never forgotten him. But not for his darling handsome face. Oh, no. What I've never forgotten is that except for Eric, I would never have known Carmella, Adelina, and Florry.

# From *Dandelion Wine*

### Ray Bradbury

Late that night, going home from the show with his mother and father and his brother Tom, Douglas saw the tennis shoes in the bright store window. He glanced quickly away, but his ankles were seized, his feet suspended, then rushed. The earth spun; the shop awnings slammed their canvas wings overhead with the thrust of his body running. His mother and father and brother walked quietly on both sides of him. Douglas walked backward, watching the tennis shoes in the midnight window left behind.

"It was a nice movie," said Mother.

Douglas murmured, "It was . . ."

It was June and long past time for buying the special shoes that were quiet as a summer rain falling on the walks. June and the earth full of raw power and everything everywhere in motion. The grass was still pouring in from the country, surrounding the sidewalks, stranding the houses. Any moment the town would capsize, go down and leave not a stir in the clover and weeds. And here Douglas stood, trapped on the dead cement and the red-brick streets, hardly able to move.

"Dad!" He blurted it out. "Back there in that window, those Cream-Sponge Para Litefoot Shoes . . ."

His father didn't even turn. "Suppose you tell me why you need a new pair of sneakers. Can you do that?"

"Well . . ."

It was because they felt the way it feels every summer when you take off your shoes for the first time and run in the grass. They felt like it feels sticking your feet out of the hot covers in wintertime to let the cold wind from the open window blow on them suddenly and you let them stay out a long time until you pull them back in under the covers again to feel them, like packed snow. The tennis shoes felt like it always feels the first time every year wading in the slow waters of the creek and seeing your feet below, half an inch further downstream, with refraction, than the real part of you above water.

"Dad," said Douglas, "it's hard to explain."

Somehow the people who made tennis shoes knew what boys needed and wanted. They put marshmallows and coiled springs in the soles and they wove the rest out of grasses bleached and fired in the wilderness. Somewhere deep in the soft loam of the shoes the thin hard sinews of the buck deer were hidden. The people that made the shoes must have watched a lot of winds blow the trees and a lot of rivers going down to the lakes. Whatever it was, it was in the shoes, and it was summer.

Douglas tried to get all this in words.

"Yes," said Father, "but what's wrong with last year's sneakers? Why can't you dig *them* out of the closet?"

Well, he felt sorry for boys who lived in California, where they wore tennis shoes all year and never knew what it was to get winter off your feet, peel off the iron leather shoes all full of snow and rain and run barefoot for a day and then lace on the first new tennis shoes of the season, which was better than barefoot. The magic was always in the new pair of shoes. The magic night might die by the first of September, but now in late June there was still plenty of magic, and shoes like these could jump you over trees and rivers and houses. And if you wanted, they could jump you over fences and sidewalks and dogs.

"Don't you see?" said Douglas. "I just *can't* use last year's pair."

For last year's pair were dead inside. They had been fine when he started them out, last year. But by the end of summer, every year, you always found out, you always knew, you couldn't really jump over rivers and trees and houses in them, and they were dead. But this was a new year, and he felt that this time, with this new pair of shoes, he could do anything, anything at all.

They walked up on the steps to their house. "Save your money," said Dad. "In five or six weeks — "

"Summer'll be over!"

Lights out, with Tom asleep, Douglas lay watching his feet, far away down there at the end of the bed in the moonlight, free of the heavy iron shoes, the big chunks of winter fallen away from them.

"Reasons. I've got to think of reasons for the shoes."

Well, as anyone knew, the hills around town were wild with friends putting cows to riot, playing barometer to the atmospheric changes, taking sun, peeling like calendars each day to take more sun. To catch those friends, you must run much faster than foxes or squirrels. As for the town, it steamed with enemies grown irritable with heat, so remembering every winter argument and insult. *Find friends, ditch enemies!* That was the Cream-Sponge Para Litefoot motto. *Does the world run too fast? Want to catch up? Want to be alert, stay alert? Litefoot, then! Litefoot!*

He held his coin bank up and heard the faint small tinkling, the airy weight of money there.

Whatever you want, he thought, you got to make your own way. During the night now, let's find that path through the forest. . . .

Downtown, the store lights went out, one by one. A wind blew in the window. It was like a river going downstream and his feet wanting to go with it.

In his dreams he heard a rabbit running running running in the deep warm grass.

Old Mr. Sanderson moved through his shoe store as the proprietor of a pet shop must move through his shop where are kenneled animals from everywhere in the world, touching each one briefly along the way. Mr. Sanderson brushed his hands over the shoes in the window, and some of them were like cats to him and some were like dogs; he touched each pair with concern, adjusting laces, fixing tongues. Then he stood in the exact center of the carpet and looked around, nodding.

There was a sound of growing thunder.

One moment, the door to Sanderson's Shoe Emporium was empty. The next, Douglas Spaulding stood clumsily there, staring down at his leather shoes as if these heavy things could not be pulled up out of the cement. The thunder had stopped when his shoes stopped. Now, with painful slowness, daring to look only at the money in his cupped hand, Douglas moved out of the bright sunlight of Saturday noon. He made careful stacks of nickels, dimes, and quarters on the counter, like someone playing chess and worried if the next move carried him out into sun or deep into shadow.

"Don't say a word!" said Mr. Sanderson.

Douglas froze.

"First, I know just what you want to buy," said Mr. Sanderson. "Second, I see you every afternoon at my window; you think I don't see? You're wrong. Third, to give it its full name, you want the Royal Crown Cream-Sponge Para Litefoot Tennis Shoes: 'LIKE MENTHOL ON YOUR FEET!' Fourth, you want credit."

"No!" cried Douglas, breathing hard, as if he'd run all night in his dreams. "I got something better than credit to offer!" he gasped. "Before I tell, Mr. Sanderson, you got to do me one small favor. Can you remember when was the last time you yourself wore a pair of Litefoot sneakers, sir?"

Mr. Sanderson's face darkened. "Oh, ten, twenty, say, thirty years ago. Why . . . ?"

"Mr. Sanderson, don't you think you owe it to your customers, sir, to at least try the tennis shoes you sell, for just one minute, so you know how they feel? People forget if they don't keep testing things. United Cigar Store man smokes cigars, don't he? Candy-store man samples his own stuff, I should think. So . . ."

"You may have noticed," said the old man, "I'm wearing shoes."

"But not sneakers, sir! How you going to sell sneakers unless you can rave about them and how you going to rave about them unless you know them?"

Mr. Sanderson backed off a little distance from the boy's fever, one hand to his chin. "Well . . ."

"Mr. Sanderson," said Douglas, "you sell me something and I'll sell you something just as valuable."

"Is it absolutely necessary to the sale that I put on a pair of the sneakers, boy?" said the old man.

"I sure wish you could, sir!"

The old man sighed. A minute later, seated panting quietly, he laced the tennis shoes to his long narrow feet. They looked detached and alien down there next to the dark cuffs of his business suit. Mr. Sanderson stood up.

"How do they *feel?*" asked the boy.

"How do they feel, he asks; they feel fine." He started to sit down.

"Please!" Douglas held out his hand. "Mr. Sanderson, now could you kind of rock back and forth a little, sponge around, bounce kind of, while I tell you the rest? It's this: I give you my money, you give me the shoes, I owe you a dollar. But, Mr. Sanderson, *but* — soon as I get those shoes on, you know what *happens?*"

"What?"

"Bang! I deliver your packages, pick up packages, bring you coffee, burn your trash, run to the post office, telegraph office, library! You'll see twelve of me in and out, in and out, every minute. Feel those shoes, Mr. Sanderson, *feel* how fast they'd take me? All those springs inside? Feel all the running inside? Feel how they kind of grab hold and can't let you alone and don't like you just *standing* there? Feel how quick I'd be doing the things you'd rather not bother with? You stay in the nice cool store while I'm jumping all around town! But it's not me really, it's the shoes. They're going like mad down alleys, cutting corners, and back! There they go!"

Mr. Sanderson stood amazed with the rush of words. When the words got going the flow carried him; he began to sink deep in the shoes, to flex his toes, limber his arches, test his ankles. He rocked softly, secretly, back and forth in a small breeze from the open door. The tennis shoes silently hushed themselves deep in the carpet, sank as in a jungle grass, in loam and resilient clay. He gave one solemn bounce of his heels in the yeasty dough, in the yielding and welcoming earth. Emotions hurried over his face as if many colored lights had been switched on and off. His mouth hung slightly open. Slowly he gentled and rocked himself to a halt, and the boy's voice faded and they stood there looking at each other in a tremendous and natural silence.

A few people drifted by on the sidewalk outside, in the hot sun.

Still the man and boy stood there, the boy glowing, the man with revelation in his face.

"Boy," said the old man at last, "in five years, how would you like a job selling shoes in this emporium?"

"Gosh, thanks, Mr. Sanderson, but I don't know what I'm going to be yet."

"Anything you want to be, son," said the old man, "you'll be. No one will ever stop you."

The old man walked lightly across the store to the wall of ten thousand boxes, came back with some shoes for the boy, and wrote up a list on some paper while the boy was lacing the shoes on his feet and then standing there, waiting.

The old man held out his list. "A dozen things you got to do for me this afternoon. Finish them, we're even Stephen, and you're fired."

"Thanks, Mr. Sanderson!" Douglas bounded away.

"Stop!" cried the old man.

Douglas pulled up and turned.

Mr. Sanderson leaned forward. "How do they *feel?*"

The boy looked down at his feet deep in the rivers, in the fields of wheat, in the wind that already was rushing him out of the town. He looked up at the old man, his eyes burning, his mouth moving, but no sound came out.

"Antelopes?" said the old man, looking from the boy's face to his shoes. "Gazelles?"

The boy thought about it, hesitated, and nodded a quick nod. Almost immediately he vanished. He just spun about with a whisper and went off. The door stood empty. The sound of the tennis shoes faded in the jungle heat.

Mr. Sanderson stood in the sun-blazed door, listening. From a long time ago, when he dreamed as a boy, he remembered the sound. Beautiful creatures leaping under the sky, gone through brush, under trees, away, and only the soft echo their running left behind.

"Antelopes," said Mr. Sanderson. "Gazelles."

He bent to pick up the boy's abandoned winter shoes, heavy with forgotten rains and long-melted snows. Moving out of the blazing sun, walking softly, lightly, slowly, he headed back toward civilization. . . .

# Be-ers and Doers

## Budge Wilson

Mom was a little narrow wisp of a woman. You wouldn't have thought to look at her that she could move a card table; even for me it was sometimes hard to believe the ease with which she could shove around an entire family. Often I tried to explain her to myself. She had been brought up on the South Shore of Nova Scotia. I wondered sometimes if the scenery down there had rubbed off on her — all those granite rocks and fogs and screeching gulls, the slow, laboring springs, and the quick, grudging summers. And then the winters — grayer than doom, and endless.

I was the oldest. I was around that house for five years before Maudie came along. They were peaceful, those five years, and even now it's easy to remember how everything seemed calm and simple. But now I know why. I was a conformist and malleable as early as three years old; I didn't buck the system. If Mom said, "Hurry, Adelaide!" If she said to me, at five, "Fold that laundry, now, Adie, and don't let no grass grow under your feet," I folded it fast. So there were very few battles at first, and no major wars.

Dad, now, he was peaceful just by nature. If a tornado had come whirling in the front door and lifted the roof clear off its hinges, he probably would have just scratched the back of his neck and said, with a kind of slow surprise, "Well! Oho! Just think o' that!" He had been born in the Annapolis Valley, where the hills are round and gentle, and the summers sunlit and very warm.

"Look at your father!" Mom would say to us later. "He thinks that all he's gotta do is *be*. Well, bein' ain't good enough. You gotta *do,* too. Me, I'm a doer." All the time she was talking, she'd be knitting up a storm, or mixing dough, or pushing a mop — hands forever and ever on the move.

Although Mom was fond of pointing out to us the things our father didn't do, he must have been doing something. Our farm was in the most fertile part of the valley, and it's true that we had the kind of soil that seemed to make things grow all of their own accord. Those beets and carrots and potatoes just came pushing up into the sunshine with an effortless grace, and they kept us well fed, with plenty left over to sell. But there was weeding and harvesting to do, and all those ten cows to milk — not to mention the thirty apple trees in our orchard to be cared for. I think maybe he just did his work so slowly and quietly that she found it hard to believe he was doing anything at all. Besides, on the South Shore, nothing ever grew without a struggle. And when Dad was through all his chores, or in between times, he liked to just sit on our old porch swing and watch the spring unfold or the summer blossom. And in the fall, he sat there smiling, admiring the rows of vegetables, the giant sunflowers, the golden leaves gathering in the trees of North Mountain.

Maudie wasn't Maudie for the reasons a person is a Ginny or a Gertie or a Susie. She wasn't called Maudie because she was cute. She got that name because if you've got a terrible name like Maud, you have to do something to rescue it. She was called after Mom's aunt Maud, who was a miser and had the whole Bank of Nova Scotia under her mattress. But she was a crabby old thing who just sat around living on her dead husband's stocks and bonds. A be-er, not a doer. Mom really scorned Aunt Maud and hated her name, but she had high hopes that our family would sometime cash in on that gold mine under the mattress. She hadn't counted on Aunt Maud going to Florida one winter and leaving her house in the care of a dear old friend. The dear old friend emptied the contents of the mattress, located Aunt Maud's three diamond rings, and took off for Mexico, leaving the pipes to freeze and the cat to die of starvation. After that, old Aunt Maud couldn't have cared less if everybody in the whole district had been named after her. She was that bitter.

Maudie was so like Mom that it was just as if she'd been cut out with a cookie cutter from the same dough. Raced around at top speed all through her growing-up time, full of projects and sports and hobbies and gossip and nerves. And mad at everyone who sang a different tune.

But this story's not about Maudie. I guess you could say it's mostly about Albert.

Albert was the baby. I was eight years old when he was born, and I often felt like he was my own child. He was special to all of us, I guess, except maybe to Maudie, and when Mom saw him for the first time, I watched a slow soft tenderness in her face that was a rare thing for any of us to see. I was okay because I was cooperative, and I knew she loved me. Maudie was her clone, and almost like a piece of herself, so they admired one another, although they were too similar to be at peace for very long. But Albert was something different. Right away, I knew she was going to pour into Albert something that didn't reach the rest of us, except in part. As time went on, this scared me. I could see that she'd made up her mind that Albert was going to be a perfect son. That meant, among other things, that he was going to be a fast-moving doer. And even when he was three or four, it wasn't hard for me to know that this wasn't going to be easy. Because Albert was a be-er. *Born* that way.

As the years went by, people around Wilmot used to say, "Just look at that family of Hortons. Mrs. Horton made one child — Maudie. Then there's Adelaide, who's her own self. But Albert, now. Mr. Horton made him all by himself. They're alike as two pine needles."

And just as nice, I could have added. But Mom wasn't either pleased or amused. "You're a bad influence on that boy, Stanley," she'd say to my dad. "How's he gonna get any ambition if all he sees is a father who can spend up to an hour leanin' on his hoe, starin' at the Mountain?" Mom had it all worked out that Albert was going to be a lawyer or a doctor or a Member of Parliament.

My dad didn't argue with her, or at least not in an angry way, "Aw, c'mon now, Dorothy," he might say to her, real slow. "The vegetables are comin' along jest fine. No need to shove them more than necessary. It does a man good to look at them hills. You wanta try it sometime. They tell you things."

"Nothin' *I* need t'hear," she'd huff, and disappear into the house, clattering pans, thumping the mop, scraping the kitchen table across the floor to get at more dust. And Albert would just watch it all, saying not a word, chewing on a piece of grass.

Mom really loved my dad, even though he drove her nearly crazy. Lots more went on than just nagging and complaining. If you looked really hard, you could see that. If it hadn't been for Albert and wanting him to be a four-star son, she mightn't have bothered to make Dad look so useless. Even so, when they sat on the swing together at night, you could feel their closeness. They didn't hold hands or anything. Her hands were always too busy embroidering, crocheting, mending something, or just swatting mosquitoes. But they liked to be together. Personal chemistry, I thought as I grew older, is a mysterious and contrary thing.

One day, Albert brought his report card home from school, and Mom looked at it hard and anxious, eyebrows knotted. " 'Albert seems a nice child,' " she read aloud to all of us, more loudly than necessary, " 'but his marks could be better. He spends too much time looking out the window, dreaming.' " She paused. No one spoke.

"Leanin' on his hoe," continued Mom testily. "Albert!" she snapped at him. "You pull up your socks by Easter or you're gonna be in deep trouble."

Dad stirred uneasily in his chair. "Aw, Dorothy," he mumbled. "Leave him be. He's a good kid."

"Or could be. *Maybe*," she threw back at him. "What he seems like to me is rock-bottom lazy. He sure is slow-moving, and could be he's slow in the head, too. Dumb."

Albert's eyes flickered at that word, but that's all. He just stood there and watched, eyes level.

"But I love him a lot," continued Mom, "and unlike you, I don't plan t'just sit around and watch him grow dumber. If it's the last thing I do, I'm gonna light a fire under his feet."

Albert was twelve then, and the nagging began to accelerate in earnest.

"How come you got a low mark in your math test?"

"I don't like math. It seems like my head don't want it."

"But do you *work* at it?"

"Well, no. Not much. Can't see no sense in workin' hard at something I'll never use. I can add up our grocery bill. I pass. That's enough."

"Not for me, it ain't," she'd storm back at him. "No baseball practice for you until you get them sums perfect. Ask Maudie t'check them." Maudie used to drum that arithmetic into him night after night. She loved playing schoolteacher, and that's how she eventually ended up. And a cross one.

One thing Albert was good at, though, was English class. By the time he got to high school, he spent almost as much time reading as he did staring into space. His way of speaking changed. He stopped dropping his *g*'s. He said *isn't* instead of *ain't*. His tenses were all neated up. He wasn't putting on airs. I just think that all those people in his books started being more real to him than his own neighbors. He loved animals, too. He made friends with the calves and even the cows. Mutt and Jeff, our two gray cats, slept on his bed every night. Often you could see him out in the fields, talking to our dog, while he was working.

"Always messin' around with animals," complained Mom. "Sometimes I think he's three parts woman and one part child. He's fifteen years old, and last week I caught him bawlin' in the hayloft after we had to shoot that male calf. Couldn't understand why y' can't go on feedin' an animal that'll never produce milk."

"Nothing wrong with liking animals," I argued. I was home for the weekend from my secretarial job in Wolfville.

"Talkin' to dogs and cryin' over cattle is not what I'd call a shortcut to success. And the cats spend so much time with him that they've forgotten why we brought them into the house in the first place. For mice."

"Maybe there's more to life than success or mice," I said. I was twenty-three now, and more interested in Albert than in conformity.

Mom made a "huh" sound through her nose. "Adelaide Horton," she said, "when you're my age, you'll understand more about success and mice than you do now. Or the lack of them." She turned on her heel and went back in the house. "And if you can't see," she said through the screen door, "why I don't want Albert to end up exactly like your father, then you've got even less sense than I thought you had. I don't want any son of mine goin' through life just satisfied to *be*." Then I could hear her banging around in the kitchen.

I looked off the verandah out at the front field, where Dad and Albert were raking up hay for the cattle, slowly, with lots of pauses for talk. All of a sudden they stopped, and Albert pointed up to the sky. It was fall, and four long wedges of geese were flying far above us, casting down their strange muffled cry. The sky was cornflower blue, and the wind was sending white clouds scudding across it. My breath was caught with the beauty of it all, and as I looked at Dad and Albert, they threw away their rakes and lay down flat on their backs, right there in the front pasture, in order to drink in the sky. And after all the geese had passed over, they stayed like that for maybe twenty minutes more.

We were all home for Christmas the year Albert turned eighteen. Maudie was having her Christmas break from teaching, and she was looking skinnier and more tight-lipped than I remembered her. I was there with my husband and my new baby, Jennifer, and Albert was even quieter than usual. But content, I thought. Not making any waves. Mom had intensified her big campaign to have him go to Acadia University in the fall. "Pre-law," she said, "or maybe teacher training. Anyways, you gotta go. A man has to be successful." She avoided my father's eyes. "In the fall," she said. "For sure."

"It's Christmas," said Dad, without anger. "Let's just be happy and forget all them plans for a few days." He was sitting at the kitchen table breaking up the bread slowly, slowly, for the turkey stuffing. He chuckled. "I've decided to be a doer this Christmas."

"And if the doin's bein' done at that speed," she said, taking the bowl from him, "we'll be eatin' Christmas dinner on New Year's Day." She started to break up the bread so quickly that you could hardly focus on her flying fingers.

Christmas came and went. It was a pleasant time. The food was good; Jennifer slept right through dinner and didn't cry all day. We listened to the Queen's Christmas message; we opened presents. Dad gave Mom a ring with a tiny sapphire in it, although she'd asked for a new vacuum cleaner.

"I like this better," she said, and looked as though she might cry.

"We'll get the vacuum cleaner in January," he said, "That's no kind of gift to get for Christmas. It's a work thing."

She looked as if she might say something, but she didn't.

It was on December 26th that it happened. That was the day of the fire.

It was a lazy day. We all got up late, except me, of course, who had to feed the baby at two and at six. But when we were all up, we just sort of lazed around in our dressing gowns, drinking coffee, admiring one anothers' presents, talking about old times, singing a carol or two around the old organ. Dad had that look on him that he used to get when all his children were in his house at the same time. Like he was in temporary possession of the best that life had to offer. Even Mom was softened up, and she sat by the grate fire and talked a bit, although there was still a lot of jumping up and down and rushing out to the kitchen to check the stove or cut up vegetables. Me, I think that on the day after Christmas you should just eat up leftovers and enjoy a slow state of collapse. But you can't blame a person for feeding you. It's handy to have a Martha or two around a house that's already equipped with three Marys. Albert was the best one to watch, though. To me, anyway. He was sitting on the floor in his striped pajamas, holding Jennifer, rocking her, and singing songs to her in a low, crooning voice. Tender, I thought, the way I like a man to be.

Albert had just put the baby back in her carriage when a giant spark flew out of the fireplace. It hit the old nylon carpet like an incendiary bomb, and the rug burst into flames. Mom started waving an old afghan over it, as though she was blowing out a match, but all she was doing was fanning the fire.

While most of us stood there in immovable fear, Albert had already grabbed Jennifer, carriage and all, and rushed out to the barn with her. He was back in a flash, just in time to see Maudie's dressing gown catch fire. He pushed her down on the floor and lay on top of her to smother the flames, and then he was up on his feet again, taking charge.

"Those four buckets in the summer kitchen!" he yelled. "Start filling them!" He pointed to Mom and Dad, who obeyed him like he was a general and they were the privates. To my husband he roared, "Get out to th' barn and keep that baby warm!"

"And you!" He pointed to me. "Call the fire department. It's 825-3131." In the meantime, the smoke was starting to fill the room and we were all coughing. Little spits of fire were crawling up the curtains, and Maudie was just standing there, shrieking.

Before Mom and Dad got back with the water, Albert was out in the back bedroom hauling up the carpet. Racing in with it over his shoulder, he bellowed, "Get out o' the way!" and we all moved. Then he slapped the carpet over the flames on the floor, and the fire just died without so much as a pro-test. Next he grabbed one of the big cushions off the sofa, and chased around after the little lapping flames on curtains and chairs and table runners, smothering them. When Mom and Dad appeared with a bucket in each hand, he shouted, "Stop! Don't use that stuff! No need t'have water damage too!"

Then Albert was suddenly still, hands hanging at his sides with the fingers spread. He smiled shyly.

"It's out," he said.

I rushed up and hugged him, wailing like a baby, loving him, thanking him. For protecting Jennifer — from smoke, from fire, from cold, from heaven knows what. Everyone opened windows and doors, and before too long, even the smoke was gone. It smelled pretty awful, but no one cared.

When we all gathered again in the parlor to clear up the mess, and Jennifer was back in my bedroom asleep, Mom stood up and looked at Albert, her eyes ablaze with admiration — and with something else I couldn't put my finger on.

"Albert!" she breathed. "We all thank you! You've saved the house, the baby, all of us, even our Christmas presents. I'm proud, proud, *proud* of you."

Albert just stood there, smiling quietly, but very pale. His hands were getting red and sort of puckered looking.

Mom took a deep breath. "And *that*," she went on, "is what I've been looking for, all of your life. Some sort of a sign that you were one hundred percent alive. And now we all know you are. Maybe even a lick more alive than the rest of us. So!" She folded her arms, and her eyes bored into him. "I'll have no more excuses from you now. No one who can put out a house fire single-handed and rescue a niece and a sister and organize us all into a fire brigade is gonna sit around for the rest of his life gatherin' dust. No siree! Or leanin' against no hoe. Why, you even had the fire department number tucked away in your head. Just imagine what you're gonna be able to do with them kind o' brains! I'll never, never rest until I see you educated and successful. Doin' what you was meant to do. I'm just proud of you, Albert. So terrible proud!"

Members of the fire department were starting to arrive at the front door, but Albert ignored them. He was white now, like death, and he made a low and terrible sound. He didn't exactly pull his lips back from his teeth and growl, but the result was similar. It was like the sound a dog makes before he leaps for the throat. And what he said was "*You jest leave me be, woman!*"

We'd never heard words like this coming out of Albert, and the parlor was as still as night as we all listened.

"You ain't proud o' me, Mom," he whispered, all his beautiful grammar gone. "Yer jest proud o' what you want me t'be. And I got some news for you. Things I shoulda tole you years gone by. *I ain't gonna be what you want.*" His voice was starting to quaver now, and he was trembling all over. "*I'm gonna be me.* And it seems like if that's ever gonna happen, it'll have t'be in some other place. And I plan t'do somethin' about that before the day is out."

Then he shut his eyes and fainted right down onto the charred carpet. The firemen carted him off to the hospital, where he was treated for shock and second-degree burns. He was there for three weeks.

My dad died of a stroke when he was sixty-six. "Not enough exercise," said Mom, after she'd got over the worst part of her grief. "Too much sittin' around watchin' the lilacs grow. No way for his blood to circulate good." Me, I ask myself if he just piled up his silent tensions until he burst wide open. Maybe he wasn't all that calm and peaceful after all. Could be he was just waiting, like Albert, for the moment when it would all come pouring out. Perhaps that wasn't the way it was; but all the same, I wonder.

Mom's still going strong at eighty-eight. Unlike Dad's, her blood must circulate like a racing stream, what with all that rushing around; she continues to move as if she's being chased. She's still knitting and preserving and scrubbing and mending and preaching. She'll never get one of those tension diseases like angina or cancer or even arthritis, because she doesn't keep one single thing bottled up inside her for more than five minutes. Out it all comes like air out of a flat tire — with either a hiss or a bang.

Perhaps it wasn't growing up on the South Shore that made Mom the way she is. I live on that coast now, and I've learned that it's more than just gray and stormy. I know about the long sandy beaches and the peace that comes of a clear horizon. I've seen the razzle-dazzle colors of the low-lying scarlet bushes in the fall, blazing against the black of the spruce trees and the bluest sky in the world. I'm familiar with the way one single radiant summer day can make you forget a whole fortnight of fog — like birth after a long labor. You might say that the breakers out on the reefs are angry or full of threats. To me, though, those waves are leaping and dancing, wild with freedom and joyfulness. But I think Mom was in a hurry from the moment she was born. I doubt if she ever stopped long enough to take notice of things like that.

Albert left home as soon as he got out of the hospital. He worked as a stevedore in Halifax for a number of years, and when he got enough money saved, he bought a little run-down house close to Digby, with a view of the Bay of Fundy. He's got a small chunk of land that's so black and rich that it doesn't take any pushing at all to make the flowers and vegetables grow. He has a cow and a beagle and four cats — and about five hundred books. He fixes lawn mowers and boat engines for the people in his area, and he putters away at his funny little house. He writes pieces for the *Digby Courier* and the *Novascotian,* and last winter he confessed to me that he writes poetry. He's child-less and wifeless, but he has the time of day for any kid who comes around to hear stories or to have a broken toy fixed. He keeps an old rocker out on the edge of the cliff, where he can sit and watch the tides of Fundy rise and fall.

# Notes on Contributors

Vivien Alcock has written many outstanding books for young readers, including *The Monster Garden, Travelers by Night,* and *The Cuckoo Sister.* She lives in London with her husband, writer Leon Garfield.

Ray Bradbury has crafted hundreds of stories and has written dozens of novels, including *Fahrenheit 451.* He has been writing science fiction and fantasy literature since the 1940s.

Judith Ortiz Cofer was born in Puerto Rico and lived there and in Paterson, New Jersey, as a child. She has published short stories for both children and adults. Ms. Cofer teaches English and creative writing at the University of Georgia.

Borden Deal lived through the Depression and frequently wrote about that period and the South in his more than twenty novels, including *Least One,* and one hundred short stories. "Antaeus," like many of his stories, deals with humankind's mystical attachment to the earth.

# Notes on Contributors

Michael Dorris has written many highly acclaimed novels for teens and adults; Rayona first appeared as a character in his book *A Yellow Raft in Blue Water.* He is also the author of *Morning Girl* and *Guests.*

Francisco Jiménez was born in Mexico and moved with his family to Santa Maria, California, as a migrant worker. "The Circuit" is based on this childhood experience. Mr. Jiménez is now a scholar, university professor, and author of short stories and books of literary criticism.

Cherylene Lee creates plays and poetry, and her short stories have appeared in many collections, including Laurence Yep's *American Dragons* and Jessica Hagedorn's *Charlie Chan Is Dead.*

Norma Fox Mazer has written many fine novels for young readers, including *After the Rain, Taking Terri Mueller,* and *Downtown.*

Although he once delivered newspapers and flipped hamburgers at McDonalds, Peter D. Sieruta now works for the Wayne State University Libraries, in Detroit, Michigan. He has written short stories — some of which are collected in *Heartbeats and Other Stories* — as well as criticism of children's and young adult books.

Gary Soto was born in Fresno, California, the setting for "The No-Guitar Blues." He writes poetry and narrative prose. Among his books are *Neighborhood Odes* and *The Skirt.*

Budge Wilson lives in Hubbards, Nova Scotia; her work has appeared in numerous anthologies. She is also the author of *The Dandelion Garden.*

Tim Wynne-Jones lives in eastern Ontario, Canada. In addition to his books for children and adults, he has written a libretto for an opera and a children's musical; he also creates music for his rock band, The Suspects.

# Copyright
# Acknowledgments

# Copyright Acknowledgments